184 1

"*I won't sugarcoat reality with a lot of romantic ballyhoo.*"

"All women are not like her, Bennet," Maggie whispered, reaching up to frame his jaw with cool, alluring fingertips.

"Aren't they?" he rumbled, his lips exploring her temples and straying down her cheek to her throat.

Her reply almost got lost between one ragged breath and the next. "No ... !"

"Make me believe you," he demanded hoarsely before he pressed his lips against hers.

CATHERINE SPENCER suggests she turned to romance-fiction writing to keep from meddling in the love lives of her five daughters and two sons. The idea was that she would keep herself busy manipulating the characters in her novels instead. This, she says, has made everyone happy. In addition to writing novels, Catherine Spencer also plays the piano, collects antiques and grows tropical shrubs at her home in Vancouver, B.C., Canada.

Books by Catherine Spencer

HARLEQUIN PRESENTS
1406—THE LOVING TOUCH
1587—NATURALLY LOVING

HARLEQUIN ROMANCE
3138—WINTER ROSES

Don't miss any of our special offers. Write to us at the following address for information on our newest releases.

Harlequin Reader Service
P.O. Box 1397, Buffalo, NY 14240
Canadian address: P.O. Box 603,
Fort Erie, Ont. L2A 5X3

CATHERINE SPENCER

DEAR MISS JONES

Harlequin Books

TORONTO • NEW YORK • LONDON
AMSTERDAM • PARIS • SYDNEY • HAMBURG
STOCKHOLM • ATHENS • TOKYO • MILAN
MADRID • WARSAW • BUDAPEST • AUCKLAND

FOR ANNE AND BOB,
WITH ADMIRATION AND RESPECT

ISBN 0-373-11623-3

DEAR MISS JONES

CHAPTER ONE

SUNLIGHT glanced off the paned windows, blinding her for a moment too long. Beneath her feet, a film of moss turned the paving stones treacherous. Crazily, the fir trees, which had remained firmly rooted for a hundred years or more, swung their branches sideways across her line of vision, and something crunched unpleasantly against the back of her head. Then stars exploded, bright red and pink, and she heard the magnified sound of someone breathing close to her face.

She blinked, winced at how painful such a tiny movement could be, and looked up. Saw yellow gold eyes, a long, inquisitive nose, black hair. And fangs.

Just for a second, time ran backward and she cringed inside her terror, waiting. Damp breath whiffled over her face. She heard the approach of human footsteps and braced herself for the sound of Eric's voice taunting her with sadistic malice, egging on the Rottweilers straining at their steel chains.

"Down, Beau!" a voice commanded lazily.

Dazed, she opened her eyes again. Another face had joined the first. Pewter gray eyes, this time, their irises ringed in charcoal. Not nearly as much hair, not quite as black, and no fangs. As for the nose with its imperious aquiline bridge, it might have been inherited from Caesar himself.

A vague sense of familiarity assailed her, then was gone.

Fingers probed the tender spot at the base of her skull and the next moment she found herself cradled against a firm shoulder. The world tilted again, except that this time she floated up instead of crashing down. Whoever he was, he was very tall, impressively strong, and he was not Eric.

He carried her as if she were a child. Indeed, he spoke to her as if she were, too. "You've got quite a goose egg," he observed, swinging up steps and through a front door that creaked on its hinges, "and you've only got yourself to blame. Unless, of course, you can't read."

Time hadn't played tricks, after all! This was not Philadelphia, and she was no longer Mrs. Eric Carlson-Lewis III. Relief made her bold. "If you're referring to the No Trespassing sign, I hardly expected it applied to me."

"An unfortunate assumption," he retorted, carrying her into a room on the left of the front hall. "I'm a man who values privacy over all else, and I particularly dislike people who drop in uninvited."

As if to lend emphasis to his words, he deposited her rather ungently on a couch beside the empty hearth. "Now lie still while I get the first-aid kit."

"I'm quite all right," she said, and made a move to sit up, intending to introduce herself. Annoyingly, a wave of dizziness overcame her, and she clutched at the arm of the couch.

"I said, lie still! I don't want blood all over the upholstery." Halfway to the door, he stopped and looked back at her, his expression a mixture of exasperation and concern. "I suppose you'd like a cup of tea to settle your nerves."

Less a question than an irritable observation on the vagaries of women, the remark did little to endear him to her. "Yes," she said. "It's the least you can do, all things considered."

Strongly marked brows rose above the cool, gray eyes. "Really? I fail to see why."

"You invited me to come here."

"I—?" He looked astonished, then incredulous. "*You're* Miss Margaret Jones, the schoolteacher?"

"Well, who did you think I was?" she snapped. If he was one of those archaic men who thought teachers should be elderly and homely to qualify as capable, they were off to a very bad start.

"Beau thought you were a postal worker," he said, faint amusement underlying his words. "It's the way you're dressed, I suppose."

She looked down at her navy jumpsuit and wondered how he could possibly confuse a Paulo Savari original with Canada Post's uniform.

Following her glance, he allowed himself a smile. It softened his features and made him dangerously handsome. "Actually, it's less what you're wearing than that sack you have slung over your shoulder."

"That's my bag," she said, offended.

"Good Lord!" He raised mystified eyes toward the ceiling. "What, I wonder, constitutes your idea of a suitcase?"

He had a disconcertingly beautiful voice, far too deep and melodious for her to have mistaken it, even fleetingly, for Eric's reedy tenor. He was good-looking, too, an imposing figure, elegantly carved from well-toned muscle. Thick hair topped a face whose cheekbones and jaw were so firmly sculpted that it was easy to overlook the sensitive mouth and rather shy eyes. "I think I would like some tea," she said primly, hoping to offset the urge to gaze at him admiringly, "and then, perhaps, we could get down to business."

He straightened to a full six feet two or more. "Yes, Miss Jones, ma'am! At once. By the way, in case you haven't guessed, I'm Bennet Montgomery."

The animal, not a Rottweiler at all but a large black creature nonetheless, with long, silky fur, paced restlessly back and forth in front of her, his plume of a tail swishing. Maggie supposed that, as far as possible for a dog, he had a gentle face, but what struck her most was his size. She'd seen smaller wolves in zoos! "Before you go, Mr. Montgomery," she said, trying to disguise the tremor in her voice which she couldn't quite control, "would you please call off your hound?"

"Why?" he asked. "He lives here, and he's not bothering you."

Oh, yes, he was! "I don't like dogs," she admitted.

"Don't be tiresome." Bennet Montgomery dismissed her as casually as he might a fly. "Everyone likes dogs."

"I don't."

He came back to tower over her, the filtered light from the window shadowing his features, but the scent of male cologne, a blend of leather and sandalwood, teased her nostrils to underscore his presence. "Then we have a problem," he said.

"Why? I understood my potential student to be a boy, not a dog."

"Where Christopher goes, Beauregarde goes. It's as simple as that."

As though he knew he was being talked about, the dog sat down next to her and cocked his head to one side, ears pricked attentively. Then, without warning, he lifted a front paw and planted it on her knee, holding her prisoner. A gasp of sheer panic whistled past her lips.

At the sound, Bennet Montgomery surveyed her more narrowly, his impatience vanishing. "You're afraid of him!" he exclaimed. "Why on earth didn't you say so in the first place?"

"Because..." she began, then lapsed into silence, too ashamed to admit to a stranger that three years of marriage to Eric had turned her into such a miserable coward.

Not waiting for her to finish, Bennet snapped his fingers. Obediently, the dog abandoned his vigil over her and trotted to the door. "I'll take him away for now," his master said, "but sooner or later you're going to have to overcome this fear. He senses it, you know—animals always do—and there'll never be complete trust between the two of you until you learn to control it.''

Trust? Maggie almost laughed in his face. She'd been so long without trust that she wasn't sure she believed in it anymore. It was one luxury she had not been able to afford during her years as Eric's wife, because it was something not to be bought, and things that didn't have a dollar value simply didn't exist in that other life.

Behind her, the door clicked shut and she found herself alone with the slumbering silence of mid-afternoon. Outside, the sun tried to penetrate the overgrown foliage that screened the windows and left the driveway in permanent shade, attesting to the fact that it had been a long time since anyone had lived in the big house—long enough for a slick layer of moss to cover the steps and cause her to make such a clumsy, if dramatic appearance.

Now that her prospective employer wasn't there to disconcert her, she took closer note of her surroundings, recognizing for the first time the elegant shape of a harpsichord, and the complementary grace of a baby grand sitting at right angles to it with a metronome perched on its closed lid. Stacks of sheet music spilled carelessly over the Aubusson carpet that covered the polished oak floor, but the walls were hung with priceless antique manuscripts illuminated in gold leaf and crimson. From all appearances, Mr. Bennet Montgomery was both a collector and a musician.

Why did she feel the evidence surrounding her merely confirmed something she already knew?

Cautiously, Maggie sat up, curious to learn more about the man whose face stirred such elusive memories. His note the day before certainly hadn't hinted at any previous acquaintance.

Dear Miss Jones,

John Keyes, the school principal, recommended I contact you with regard to tutoring a four-year-old boy over the summer. If possible, please present yourself for an interview at my home on Wednesday afternoon at two o'clock so that we may discuss the possibility of such an arrangement more fully. Sincerely, Bennet Montgomery.

An entirely impersonal, thoroughly autocratic summons which offered no clues at all. She knew no one of that name.

Maggie rose to her feet and tested her balance. Although she felt quite recovered, she had no wish to make a spectacle of herself a second time that day. The room remained stationary. Encouraged, she crossed the carpet, sparing the piano only a passing glance. It was the rosewood harpsichord with its double keyboard that captured her full attention.

Intrigued, she ran her fingers over the old ivory keys and found herself picking out a tune she remembered from the piano lessons she had endured as a child. "The Waltzing Teapot" or some such title, a five-finger exercise thinly disguised as a party piece. She had hated it then, but it captivated her now, its simple theme transformed by the harpsichord into something a medieval minstrel might have plucked for his ladylove.

"Did I not make myself clear, Miss Jones?" a voice which was anything but loverlike inquired. "Or must I post No Trespassing signs inside my house as well as out, in order to preserve my privacy?"

Guiltily, Maggie snatched her fingers from the keys and spun around. Bennet Montgomery stood just inside the door, a tray in his hands. "I'm sorry," she said. "The harpsichord fascinated me, and I couldn't resist...although I'm not much of a musician, as you no doubt heard."

"I never would have guessed," he replied dryly, and inclined his head. "Perhaps now that you've satisfied your curiosity, you'd return to the couch and let me take another look at that lump on your head. Then, if you feel you must keep your hands busy, you can pour the tea while I decide if you're the sort of person I want in my house for the next two months."

Maggie decided it was time to take a stand. Handsome as sin he might be, but he wasn't getting away with that sort of arrogance. "Let us understand each other from the outset, Mr. Montgomery. First of all, my head is quite fine, thank you very much. My earlier mishap hasn't left me with brain damage, and, even if it had, I'd resent your attitude. Second, I'm here as much to decide whether or not *you're* the sort of person I'm prepared to forfeit my summer for as *you* are to decide whether or not you wish to hire me. I'm a professional schoolteacher, not an upstairs maid, and far more used to giving orders than taking them."

Obviously, no one had ever been so outspoken with him in recent history. At first, he looked thunderstruck, then, surprisingly, he laughed. "I'm sorry if I was offensive, Miss Jones. I'm afraid I'm getting crabby and overbearing in my old age."

He was also quite charming when he wanted to be, exuding the sort of confidence that only a successful man in his late thirties could possibly command. "I'll overlook it this time," she said, softening the asperity of her reply with a smile. "Why don't you tell me about your boy and what it is you'd like me to do for him, before either of us arrives at any hasty conclusions?"

"Only if you'll allow me to check your head. You really did get a rather nasty blow and I feel responsible."

She felt like telling him that his time would be better employed cleaning the moss from the steps so that the next unwary person would be spared what had befallen her, but he smiled so winningly that she found herself submitting to his request.

He came to sit beside her. "Bend your head forward," he ordered. Cupping one hand around her neck, he loosened the scarf which held her hair and sifted his fingers through the heavy strands. "I want to make sure you don't need stitches."

His touch was almost hypnotically soothing and far more pleasurable than circumstances or occasion warranted. "It was just a bump," she began. "I hardly think—oh, ouch!"

"Ah, just as I suspected." His fingers stilled. "You broke the skin, but not badly." Very gently, he swabbed at the wound with disinfectant. "You have beautiful hair, Miss Jones. It would have been a pity to have had to have cut it, but I think you'll heal well enough without, and in a few days there won't even be a scratch to show for your mishap."

Reaching for her scarf, he looped it around her hair again and tried to replace it.

"Let me—it'll slide off unless it's tied very tight—you..." Maggie raised her hands to replace his, but somehow their fingers stumbled over each other and became entangled. At the same time, her gaze connected with his and she found it impossible to look away again. Very long, very silky lashes framed eyes too dramatically beautiful to be easily forgotten, which made the notion that she'd seen him somewhere before all the more unlikely.

Certainly, he didn't recognize her, as his next question proved. "Tell me about yourself, Miss Jones," he said, removing himself a safe distance along the couch and breaking the spell. "Are you from these parts?"

"No, I was born in Niagara Falls, Ontario, but I grew up in Montreal and attended McGill University."

He looked surprised. "Then how did you end up in British Columbia, in a town as small as Sagepointe? It's a far cry from Montreal."

"I don't care for big city living," she said, and changed the subject. He was entitled to know about her professional credits, but not her private life. "Fortunately, I found a job here last year."

He looked her over speculatively. "And you don't miss the glamour? The theaters and restaurants, the nightlife?"

"They're not everyone's cup of tea," she said. "Speaking of which, how do you take yours, Mr. Montgomery?"

"Clear, with one lump." He accepted the cup she handed to him and nodded his thanks. "Mr. Keyes speaks very highly of you, Miss Jones. He tells me you have extraordinary rapport with children and that you'll be in charge of a split kindergarten-grade one class in September, which is why I'm interested in hiring you to tutor Christopher until then. He'll turn five in November and is a bright enough child, but he has . . . a few problems."

Maggie's professional instincts switched to full alert at his tone. She had thought his initial request unusual—in her experience, normal four- and five-year-olds seldom needed tutors—and it was clear from the way Bennet Montgomery had chosen his words with sudden care that he recognized his son did not fit the usual mold. "What sort of problems?"

He set down his cup. "I think it's best to let you judge for yourself. Finish your tea, and, while you do so, let me tell you what I expect from you in return for the very generous salary I'm prepared to pay you."

"Provided I agree to accept the job," she reminded him. Maggie found him a very disconcerting man, charming one minute, close to insulting the next. "Judge for yourself," he'd suggested, but he might as well have come right out and said what he really meant: "see if you can figure out the problems without any help from me." And his remark about money—it smacked of the sort of attitude she'd found so untenable in her marriage to Eric. Did all men think women were for sale if the price was right?

"I don't want Christopher to feel he's in school all summer," Bennet Montgomery went on, apparently not at all deterred by her reservations. "He hasn't had much fun in the past, and that's something I'd like to rectify. On the other hand, I think you'll agree that he needs fairly extensive, er—tutoring, so I'm basing your salary on a full five-day week. Naturally, your meals will be provided. In fact, if you wish, you could live here Monday to Friday."

She opened her mouth to object, but he forestalled her by naming an outrageously high salary, and then attempted to sweeten the deal further by adding, "And in case you're concerned about compromising your reputation, Miss Jones, I have a live-in housekeeper who occupies the upper floor of the house."

Who did he think she was, Jane Eyre? "I prefer to tutor from my own house," she said firmly. The idea of having Bennet Montgomery hovering over her every waking hour was entirely too disturbing. "I have resources at hand there to provide—"

"I'm afraid that's quite out of the question. I won't have Christopher paraded through town for everyone—" He stopped, his mouth a thin line of distress. "Miss Jones, I am a stranger here. I realize that in a community as small as this, newcomers are bound to spark local curiosity. I suppose that a certain amount of speculation and gossip is unavoidable, but I am most emphatically not the kind of man who welcomes overtures from well-meaning, inquisitive neighbors. You are much younger than I had anticipated. I hope you are equally discreet, and will respect my wishes even if you do not entirely understand what motivates them. Call me antisocial if you like, but understand from the outset that what goes on inside this house is not something to be discussed abroad."

Maggie settled her teacup in its saucer. "Dear me!" she exclaimed with undisguised irony. "How very Gothic!"

For a second time, he looked taken aback, then reluctantly smiled. "It is, isn't it?" He lifted his hands helplessly. "I'm sorry, I don't mean to sound mysterious. I'm just a very private sort of person, that's all. I promise you there are no ghosts in the attic, no skeletons in the closets, just one small boy who needs a lot of attention and something approaching a normal, stable home environment. He's been bounced around from pillar to post so much in his short life that I doubt he even knows the difference between strangers and family, which is one reason I want him here with me until he starts school in September. I want him to know this is home, to feel he belongs here.''

What a strange thing to say about one's own child! ''Sagepointe is very much a family-oriented town, Mr. Montgomery. Whatever Christopher's problems, I think you'll find people here will manage to respond sympathetically to him without in any way intruding on your privacy. And if you intend to have him join the kindergarten class in September, then sooner or later he's going to have to 'parade through town' and be seen.''

''I realize that, and I don't mean to disparage anyone. I'm sure the people hereabouts are decent, worthy individuals. However, if I choose not to invite comment by exposing Christopher to them right now, then I must insist that you, Miss Jones, support me in this and place his interests ahead of your other loyalties, at least for the duration of the summer.'' He smiled again, more winningly than ever. ''Not such an arduous request to honor, surely, so what do you say? Will you take the job?''

What had she to lose? She had no other plans for the summer, and she had to admit she was intrigued. Privately, she thought his reclusiveness would likely incite just the sort of curiosity he was so eager to avoid, but, as he'd so forthrightly pointed out, how he chose to handle his child was none of her business—up to a point.

''If I take the job,'' she told him, ''you'll have to agree not to interfere. He may be your son, Mr. Montgomery, but I'm the teacher. Inside the classroom, whether it's here or at the school, I make the rules.''

"He is not my son, he is my nephew.''

"Really?'' The unexpectedness of the revelation caught her off guard, and she was unable to cover her surprise. "Where are his parents?''

His expression, which only a second before had verged on friendly, snapped closed and shut her out. "They are not here,'' he said coldly, "and that is all you need to know at this point. I think perhaps you should meet Christopher before we take this matter any further. Who knows? I might decide, when I see how you interact with him, that you're not suitable, after all. Or you might decide you don't want the job, no matter how well paid it is.''

A highly likely probability, Maggie thought, if the child was as moody and unpredictable as his uncle. "Very well.''

She followed him down the hall to the rear of the house, where a large glass solarium let in the full afternoon sun. In the middle of the floor, the dog, Beau, lay with his nose on his paws and his eyes on the child who played beside him with a collection of toy airplanes.

Like any other four-year-old, the boy zoomed them through the air and along the floor, immersed in a make-believe world of intricate flight patterns and aerobatics beyond the scope of mortal man. Unlike any other child his age, however, the noises he muttered struck a strange, discordant note.

In a rocking chair near the glass doors that opened to the garden, a gray-haired woman sat knitting, the click of her needles the only recognizable sound in the room. When she saw Bennet enter with a visitor, she put down her work, heaved herself out of the chair, and left them alone with the child and the dog.

"That was Mrs. Marshall, my housekeeper," Bennet explained. "She was with our family years ago, and I was fortunate enough to track her down and persuade her to work for me again now. And this is Christopher. Chris, there's someone here I want you to meet."

The boy would not look at her.

Flinging her an apologetic glance, Bennet crossed to his nephew and gently tried to remove the toys from his hands. "Chris," he cajoled, "come and say hello to Miss Jones."

But the more Bennet tried to persuade him to acknowledge Maggie the more stubbornly the child fixed his attention away from her. His little body grew rigid, winding up tighter with tension.

Don't force the issue, Maggie wanted to tell Bennet, but one look at his face and she knew that two wills were already locked in opposition, leaving no room for a third.

"Enough, Christopher!" he commanded sharply, and tried to capture the hand that maneuvered one of the toy aircraft with increasing agitation.

His touch triggered the outburst that had been pending since the boy had first seen her, and the next moment the toy was indeed airborne and sailing across the room to land with a dismaying crack against one of the windows. Satisfied, Christopher then turned and stared at her.

He was the most beautiful child she had ever seen, and quite the most fragile. Blond hair, eyes so blue they were almost violet, and milk-pale skin contributed to the impression of a Botticelli angel plucked from the wall of an Italian chapel, but the noise he made might have come from an outraged troll.

Wearily, Bennet Montgomery gave up the struggle and turned to Maggie, a dull flush staining his cheeks.

As well it should! Bennet Montgomery was too intelligent a man not to know the difference between a problem and a handicap. "Why didn't you tell me?" she asked him, raising her voice over the child's shrieks.

"Because if I had, you might not have agreed to an interview. And you're looking at a desperate man, Miss Jones."

The boy's frustration approached deafening proportions. Normal conversation would have to wait. Bridging the distance that separated them, Maggie knelt down and looked the child in the eye, hoping her expression conveyed the same message as her words. "Stop that noise at once, Christopher," she said firmly, "or you and I are going to have a very serious disagreement."

Briefly, he returned her gaze, then continued to shriek unintelligible noises and, when that appeared not to impress her, he lashed out, catching her by surprise with one small fist that connected sharply with her lip. Ignoring the taste of her own blood, Maggie tucked him under one arm, carried him across the room and dumped him in the rocking chair.

She didn't hold with violence, no matter how young the source, nor was she the type to submit to abuse. Not any longer. And she'd had a lot of experience in handling temper tantrums during her years as Eriç's wife. Learning to ignore them at the same time that she controlled her own frustration was a valuable lesson she hadn't forgotten.

"You may sit there and screech to your heart's content,' she assured the child, "but don't expect us to stand by and applaud."

She spun around, prepared to sweep out of the room and take Bennet Montgomery with her, and came face-to-face with the dog instead. "As for you," she snapped, too exasperated by the whole afternoon's events to be either afraid or cautious, "you can sit and howl with him, for all I care."

Bennet appeared ready to intercede and relegate her to a less prominent role, but she was having none of that. Leaving him to trail behind, she flung open the doors to the back garden, and sailed across the patio to a lawn swing set under the shade of an apple tree.

"Well!" he murmured, settling himself next to her. "I'm impressed."

Maggie was not flattered. "Why have you wasted my time and yours with this whole charade, Mr. Montgomery?"

"Charade, Miss Jones?" He flexed his fingers and studied them carefully, as though a great deal hinged on the next few minutes. "I'm not sure I understand you."

"Then either you're very stupid, or you think I am," she said scornfully, "which only makes things worse."

"He's not usually like this," Bennet hastened to explain. "Only with strangers—he regresses then, but you'll see, he'll calm down, and then . . ."

She fixed him with a determined stare. "Christopher doesn't need a tutor, Mr. Montgomery, he needs a therapist."

"He's been seeing one, a speech therapist. I can give you all kinds of pointers on how to help him. I'm sure, if you'll just give it a try, you'll find working with him very rewarding. Think of it as a challenge—something different from the usual run of things."

Maggie shook her head and turned away, trying to dismiss the pitiful sound of the child, but it filtered through the closed doors, distorted, unintelligible and so full of lonely frustration that she could hardly bear it. "You and I both know I'm not qualified to accept this job," she said at last.

When Bennet didn't immediately respond, she thought perhaps he hadn't heard, or worse, that he didn't understand, after all. But when she turned back to look at him, she knew she'd misjudged him, not once but several times. His eyes were as bleak as a cold November morning, and she read such sorrow in his face that it was all she could do not to reach out and touch him—to try to soften his pain with the warmth of her compassion.

"Who do you recommend, then, Miss Jones?" he asked quietly.

She shrugged helplessly. Sagepointe was a tiny community. Main Street was a mere three blocks long. The nearest assessment clinic was forty miles away in Annisville. "There is no one," she said. "At least, not here."

His gaze traveled slowly over her, taking stock of her from her ankles to her chin, before sliding to her mouth and then, finally, coming to rest soulfully on her eyes. Even before he spoke, she felt the web of entrapment closing in on her.

"There is you," he said, and somehow managed to make the words as beseeching as a prayer.

CHAPTER TWO

JULY afternoons were unbearably hot up there in the high country, but the mornings were pleasantly cool, with a breeze coming in off the water to sweeten the air and sharpen the scents of summer. For that reason, Maggie usually went for her run first thing. She'd pin back her hair, tie a sweatband around her forehead, do a few warm-up stretches on the front porch, then head down the path to the road that wound around the lake.

When she'd first come to Sagepointe the summer before, people had asked her if she wanted to play in the town softball league. In the autumn, they'd invited her to join the curling team. Both times she'd declined. She wasn't a great believer in team sports. She didn't care for the aggressive attitudes they fostered. Someone always got left out. To her, it was more important for an individual to compete against himself and set personal goals. When her neighbors had seen her set off to run all by herself, they'd stopped what they were doing and come out on their porches to stare. Some had even laughed and said she didn't have the sense to come in out of the rain *or* the heat. But eventually they'd grown used to her strange city ways and seldom paid attention anymore. She was a good teacher and their children liked her, and that was really all that mattered.

So, when she turned the corner at the end of her run the morning after her interview at the big house, she was more surprised to find she had a visitor waiting for her at her little house—which came with her job—than she was to discover he was Bennet Montgomery. For a start, everyone else knew she wouldn't be home and ready for company until later in the day, and second, only a stranger would dress so elegantly to come calling, once school was closed for the summer.

As one mother had jokingly complained, she could tell the day classes ended because her children stopped wearing shoes and her vacuum cleaner was always full of sand. From July to early September, Sagepointe was a beach community, and nothing short of a wedding or a funeral during the week could persuade the residents to exchange shorts or blue jeans for their Sunday best. Bennet Montgomery, lounging on Maggie's front steps dressed in silver gray trousers and dark blue silk shirt, was as conspicuous as some sleek, exotic bird in a flock of sparrows. Edith Caverley from across the road hung half out of her front window, telephone to her ear and mouth working overtime, staring in fascination at the sight.

"For someone who deplores gossip," Maggie panted, coming to a halt at the front steps, "you're inviting plenty by showing up here at this hour of the morning."

"I had no other choice," he replied. "You rushed off yesterday before we'd finished our meeting."

"I don't know how you arrived at that conclusion, Mr. Montgomery. I thought I made it plain that I'm not the person you're looking for and that I can't accept your offer."

"And I thought *I* made it plain that if you turn me down, there is no one else, Miss Jones." He looked at her narrowly. "Why are you so adamant in your refusal? Is it the money?"

"Oh, for heaven's sake!" Maggie stripped off her sweatband and used it to mop the nape of her neck. "I don't pretend to know how old you are, but I'd venture to suggest you're well past the age where you think money can buy whatever it is you decide you want."

"As a matter of fact, it's been my experience that everything has its price." He looked her over again at his leisure, apparently less concerned with how revealing her clinging shorts and T-shirt were after a five mile workout than with the simplicity of her attire. Did he perhaps think they were all the clothes she owned—apart from her "postal" outfit—and that she could use a few extra dollars?

"I'm not for sale, Mr. Montgomery," she said flatly.

"I'm no so crass as to think you are, Miss Jones," he replied mildly. "I do, however, suspect you've jumped to the wrong conclusions about Christopher."

"He has a severe hearing impediment. In plain, layman's language, he's deaf, and no amount of tutoring is going to change that, or accomplish the miracle you seem to be expecting, before school starts in September."

"Yesterday," Bennet Montgomery remarked, leaning over the porch railing to inspect the petunias growing in the flower beds below, "my first impression was that you were a rather clumsy creature given to falling over your own feet. An unflattering and entirely inaccurate assumption, as it turns out." His gaze swiveled back to her, and this time he did notice how her clothes clung. His attention skimmed the length of her legs, took note of her hips, and settled audaciously on her breasts. "In fact, Miss Jones, you're a remarkably well put-together, coordinated young woman of obvious and considerable stamina. And Christopher hears as well as you or I."

Maggie was so flustered by his scrutiny that it took a moment or two for his last comment to register. By the time it did, his gaze had swung up to concentrate on her face and take full measure of her utter astonishment. "What?" she asked, too dumbfounded to observe polite niceties.

"I said," he repeated, enunciating his words carefully, "Christopher hears as well as you or I."

"That's impossible!" As a teacher, she knew that parents sometimes had trouble reconciling high expectations with reality where their children were concerned. Normally, she tried to lead them to acceptance of the true state of affairs more diplomatically, but this was a situation so far removed from normal that her usual professional tact deserted her. "You can't seriously believe—?"

"It isn't a matter of opinion, Miss Jones, it's an established fact. My nephew's hearing is not impaired. His speech, however, is."

"How—?"

Bennet held up one long-fingered hand and gestured toward her front door. "I'm willing to answer your questions, explain as much as is necessary, and beg for your help if I must, but not here in full view of your neighbors."

Over his shoulder, Maggie saw Edith Caverley twitch her curtains aside and crane her neck to make sure she didn't miss a blink. "I'm afraid it's a little late to worry about that, but by all means come inside." She pushed open the door and waved him toward the kitchen at the end of the hall. "Help yourself to coffee while I get changed."

If he was right about Christopher, and *if* she decided to take on the job of helping the boy, that did not mean she would submit meekly to every demand her employer felt disposed to make, no matter how accustomed he might be to getting his own way. A master-servant relationship was the last thing she would tolerate. Bennet Montgomery had caught her at a disadvantage twice already. It wouldn't happen a third time. When she emerged from her bedroom fifteen minutes later, cool from a shower and with her hair tied back, Maggie looked as much the prim schoolmarm as a tailored shirtwaist dress and flat-heeled pumps could make her.

Bennet Montgomery was not in the kitchen where she expected to find him. He had taken his coffee into the living room and made himself very much at home. He looked up as she entered, and closed the doors of the breakfront bookcase, whose contents he'd been busy examining.

"A nice room," he remarked, seeming not at all embarrassed to have been caught snooping through her things. His gaze settled thoughtfully on the Dorothea Sharp original displayed above the mantelpiece, then switched to the signed Rembrandt etching hanging over an antique escritoire in the alcove next to the fireplace. "You can learn a lot about a person by the things with which she surrounds herself."

"Really? And what do you think you've learned about me?"

He favored her with the rare smile that she found so attractive. "You're a contradiction, Miss Jones. An exotic mystery lady, masquerading as ordinary."

He was too perceptive by half. She laughed nervously. "How silly! A more ordinary, down-to-earth person you couldn't hope to find."

He raised one skeptical eyebrow. "Then you won't mind listening to me plead my case and, if you're one iota as sensible as you want me to believe, you'll agree to help my nephew."

Maggie sighed. "I suppose we may as well sit down. I have the feeling this might take some time."

Determined to keep the discussion on as impersonal and professional a footing as possible, she sat behind the desk that overlooked the back garden and waved Bennet Montgomery to the small visitor's chair opposite. The morning sun, streaming over her shoulder, illuminated his face and allowed her to detect his most fleeting expression. But he, blinded by the light, would not enjoy the same privilege with her. Inclining her head, she waited for him to speak first.

"Where do I start?" he murmured, steepling his fingers under his chin. "The beginning is so far in the past, it scarcely seems relevant any longer, and yet, I suppose, in all fairness to you, I should tell you a little bit about it."

He paused and settled himself more comfortably in the chair, sliding down so that his legs sprawled under the desk and his feet came to rest not far from where hers were placed neatly side by side. "Christopher is my brother's son," he said. "His only child, thank God. Francis is seven years younger than me, and a musician of considerable, though not extraordinary talent. He is, however, extremely handsome and so completely charming that few people, especially women, are able to resist him."

As are you, Maggie thought with shocking irrelevance, and schooled her thoughts back where they belonged. "Is he a pianist, too?"

"No. Francis plays the viola da gamba." He shook his head slightly, as though irritated by her interruption. "For reasons which need not concern you, he married a young woman who was, to put it very bluntly, a deaf-mute. She became pregnant shortly before the bloom began to wear off the marriage, and by the time Christopher was born, Francis..."

At this point, Bennet Montgomery cleared his throat as though what he had to admit next was so unpalatable that he could not bring himself to go on. Although she had intended to remain silent until he had finished all he had to say, Maggie's resolve wavered in the face of his obvious distress. "He left her?" she prompted.

Her suggestion seemed to jolt him back to the present. As if horrified to find he had confided so much to a stranger, he jerked himself fully erect in the chair, his posture and his tone, when he continued, icily remote. "The state of my brother's marriage is no longer relevant, Miss Jones. His wife died last year, and Francis elected to pursue the life of a charming, carefree bachelor, a role that spares no room for a handicapped child, whereas I am cursed with scruples to make up for what I lack in . . . charisma."

A grimace of distaste crossed his features as he uttered the last word, as though it tasted somehow unpleasant, and he spread his long fingers wide, the unconsciously graceful gesture of a man whose hands were the instruments through which he expressed himself best. "To my lasting shame, I ignored my nephew while his mother was alive, which makes his current predicament as much my fault as anyone's. The boy lived with her and shared her isolation to such an extent that, when I finally did meet him, my first impression coincided with yours. I, too, thought his hearing was impaired when, in fact, silence had been so much a part of his life that he'd never learned to speak properly. Thank God I found out differently before anymore damage was done."

Maggie didn't know who to pity the most—the mother, the child, or the man seated across from her who seemed to feel he ought to have anticipated his family's fate and redirected it. "You can scarcely hold yourself to blame, surely?" she said. "You had your own life to live, after all."

Perhaps the scorn in his eyes was directed at himself, but it flayed her to the bone. "You're a little country schoolteacher, Miss Jones, dedicated to the nurturing of young minds. You cannot possibly begin to understand the sort of life I have lived, or the indulgences I have allowed myself."

She understood a good deal more than he gave her credit for. One day, if she ever felt she knew him well enough, she would tell him he was too often fooled by appearances. What would he say, for instance, if she were to tell him that, while he talked, that elusive sense of déjà vu that had tantalized her yesterday had begun to clarify? That in fact, years before when she had been one of the idle rich whom he so obviously despised, they had both attended a glittering reception where she had been as dazzled by his brother as everyone else in the room?

It was the mention of that strange-sounding instrument, viola da gamba, that had sparked the memories and caused them to knit together. Not an avid fan of the classics herself, Maggie had attended the symphony performance reluctantly, bored by the prospect of another evening of being seen in the right place with all the right people. It hadn't mattered a rap to her that the man waving the baton so imperiously had been a maestro of international acclaim who had conducted every orchestra worthy of the name from Vienna to London, from New York to Buenos Aires. Given a choice, she'd have preferred to have attended the Elton John concert being held elsewhere in Philadelphia. The last thing she'd expected was that she'd be held captive by the performance of some obscure symphony. Yet she had been transported, as much under the spell of the conductor as the musicians themselves; for a few hours, she'd even been able to forget the husband she'd grown to fear and loathe, and the life that she found so stifling.

Too soon, the concert had been over, although for Eric the evening had only just begun. She had been embarrassed by his behavior at the reception following the recital. Eric worshiped success, which he measured by the amount of money it earned. It never occurred to him that, for some people, accomplishment and recognition were more subtly defined, which was probably why he hadn't understood the amused disdain with which the musicians had received his fawning admiration.

Maggie had seen it, though, and had wished herself a thousand miles away. In fact, she had been blending into the crowd, hoping to disassociate herself from the humiliation of her husband's performance, when one of the performers had noticed her. It had been Francis Montgomery, who played the gamba, the younger brother of the aloof maestro himself.

Before she'd had time to compose herself, he had drawn her forward and bent low to kiss her hand, his

blue eyes smiling conspiratorially into hers as though
he and she enjoyed a secret too delicious to be shared
by anyone else present. Then, he'd held his champagne glass to her lips, and tilted it so that some of its
contents trickled down her throat. "How delight-
ful," he'd murmured, "to find so unspoiled and perfect a rose among all these aging hothouse blooms."

And she had blushed and giggled like the foolish
unsophisticate she'd been at the time. She'd thought
him as handsome as a god and, for a few intoxicated
moments that owed nothing to the splash of champagne she'd consumed, she'd felt that if he'd said he
was going to fly her away on his magic carpet she'd
have believed him without a moment's hesitation.
Only then had she become aware of the celebrated
maestro who stood a little apart from the crowd and
watched the scene with thinly veiled disdain.

Bennet Montgomery's gentle irony rescued her from
memories too embarrassing to merit further indulgences. "Dear Miss Jones," he chided, "I hardly
thought my story would put you to sleep."

"I wasn't sleeping," she protested.

"Really?" he murmured. "I could have sworn you
were worlds away from me. Your lovely eyes were full
of dreams."

He wasn't as flamboyant as his brother, but his
charm was every bit as formidable in its own quiet
way. Nor was she as poised in handling it as she would
have liked. She didn't blush, the way she would have
at one time, but a secret warmth stole up inside her. It
had been rather a long time since a man had paid her

so simple and sincere a compliment. "I was merely thinking," she said.

"And what have you decided?"

It was not the time to delve too deeply into motives. It was enough that a child needed help she might be able to provide, though how successful she'd be was anybody's guess. "I'll work with your nephew, Mr. Montgomery," she told him, "but I can't guarantee I'll achieve the results you're looking for. Why don't we give the arrangement a trial run—say, until the end of July? If, at that time, we are not both satisfied with the progress made, then I think you'll have to consider bringing in more specialized outside help."

He inclined his head in agreement. "Very well."

"There is one other thing. Why are you so certain that Christopher has perfect hearing? Has he been tested by an expert?"

"He's been examined by several doctors. How expert they are..." He shrugged. "One diagnosed him as autistic, another decided he was mentally retarded, possibly as a result of injury at birth, but all agreed his hearing is not impaired. I could have told them that myself, after one day with the boy."

Either Maggie's doubts showed more than she intended, or else he was much more observant than the average man. "If you will agree to begin working with him this afternoon, Miss Jones," he said, his eyes shimmering with amusement, "perhaps I can convince you that I'm more than just a doting uncle. I have a little experiment I'd like to demonstrate to you."

If, by that, he had hoped to pique her curiosity, he'd succeeded.

"What time would you like me to start, Mr. Montgomery?"

"At two o'clock. And my name, by the way, is Bennet."

Temptation flared, but she thrust it away. Keep it simple and keep it professional, she reminded herself. "Mine is Miss Jones," she replied, "and, as I expect to be your nephew's teacher for the next few months, I prefer to keep our association fairly formal. It's easier to be completely honest that way."

It was an exaggeration, of course, if not an outright lie. Half the people in town called her Maggie, and she managed to preserve her professional integrity with *them*. But none of them gave her secret flutters the way Bennet Montgomery did.

Fortunately, he couldn't read her thoughts. "Dear me!" he murmured in perfect parody of her response to him, the afternoon before. "How very Victorian!"

His "experiment" was poignantly conclusive. When she arrived at the big house, he ushered her into the music room, where the child sat on a bench before the piano. "We thought you might enjoy a little concert, Miss Jones," Bennet Montgomery said, and took a seat beside his nephew.

Maggie perched on the edge of the couch, prepared to be suitably enthusiastic, but never expecting to be so moved.

First of all, Bennet set the metronome in motion. "Listen to the conductor, Chris," he instructed, and, for a few seconds, they sat without moving. Then, very quietly, the man picked out the opening bars of a simple melody. At once, the child repeated them, an octave or two higher on the keyboard. In the background the metronome kept syncopated time, a delicate counterpoint to their duet.

With no perceptible pause, Bennet shifted key. The boy's imitation was flawless and immediate. The master introduced a little flourish; the student echoed it. Above the child's head, Bennet's eyes met Maggie's. "Prepare to be impressed," he said, and swung into a toe-tapping bass accompaniment to his partner's treble theme.

She was already sold, but it was the sight of the child's blond head nodding in rhythm, the swing of the small shoulders, the shy grin emerging on the solemn face, that enchanted her and stung her eyes with tears.

"Chopsticks!" Bennet commanded over the final crescendo, and boomed out basso profundo chords as Christopher attacked the keys with giggling relish.

At the concert's conclusion, Maggie burst into spontaneous applause. "That was wonderful!"

"It was, wasn't it?" Bennet agreed with unbridled pleasure, but, as though he suddenly remembered a stranger was in the room, Christopher covered his eyes and refused to look at her.

"Perhaps," she suggested quietly, "this young man and I need to spend a little time alone getting to know each other."

"I just remembered an important phone call I have to make," Bennet replied accommodatingly, and stood up.

The child immediately slipped down from the bench, also. Anticipating an outburst similar to the one she'd witnessed yesterday, Maggie prayed for the inspiration to divert him. "I wish I could play 'Chopsticks,'" she lamented.

Halfway to the door, Bennet stopped and rolled his eyes. "Dear Miss Jones," he replied, "anyone can play 'Chopsticks,' even you."

"You overestimate my talents, Mr. Montgomery. I'm all thumbs." As casually as possible, she approached the piano, sat down, and demonstrated the truth of her statement by plunking both thumbs on middle *C*.

"I'm afraid you're quite right," Bennet conceded.

"Perhaps if someone were to teach me," she hinted, and stole a glance at the blond cherub poised for flight by her side. A faint, high-pitched sound escaped his lips, a tiny, distorted titter of amusement which, in its own way, was as much music to Maggie's ears as the concert she'd just enjoyed.

Taking a chance, she casually reached out and lifted Christopher back onto the bench. "Show me," she said, and held her breath.

At first, he clutched his hands in his lap and stared down at them. Just when she was ready to give up hope, he placed them on the keys and, exactly as his uncle had done a few minutes earlier, he played the opening notes for her, then waited for her to repeat them.

She did, and quite deliberately made a mistake. He was not deceived. Instead of proceeding to the next bar, he repeated the first and turned reproachful blue eyes on her. When she imitated him successfully, he rewarded her with such a sweet smile, she wanted to hug him. He never noticed Bennet leave the room.

There was only so long a child his age could be kept entertained playing "Chopsticks,' Maggie thought with a hint of desperation, after what seemed like the fourteenth repetition. "Time out," she begged, massaging her fingers in pretended agony. "I can't keep up with you, Christopher."

He shot her a doubtful glance and began to slide down from the piano bench. "But I'd love to see the garden," she added, grabbing him before he escaped. "Will you show me?"

For a moment or two he considered, then, "Herg," he said, in that oddly guttural tone and, disengaging himself, headed for the door. When she made no move to follow, he turned and came back to where she still sat. "Herg," he repeated, and held out his hand.

"Okay," she agreed, not understanding what he was trying to say, and not caring, either, because at least he wasn't trying to run away from her, nor was he shrieking.

He took her down the hall toward the solarium at the back of the house. There was no sign either of Bennet or the housekeeper, Mrs. Marshall. The doors to the garden stood open and, with grave self-importance, Christopher led her across the patio, down a shallow flight of steps and past a formal flower garden to where lawn sloped down to the lake. Next to the shore, weeping willows brushed graceful branches along the ground.

They were almost at the water's edge when it happened. Tugging free his hand, Christopher flung her an impish grin and raced toward the trees. In no time at all, he was hidden by the trailing branches.

"Ah!" Maggie hid a smile, understanding at last the meaning of "Herg." "You want to play hide-and-seek!"

She began looking for him in all the wrong places, talking to herself the entire time, loudly enough so that he couldn't fail to hear what she was saying. "Where did that boy get to? He was right here a minute ago. He couldn't have just vanished into thin air."

She peered under a hydrangea bush and, when that didn't turn up anything, she crawled on all fours toward the willows.

Ahead and slightly to her right, a muffled giggle emerged. "Did you hear something?" she asked a butterfly hovering near by. "I could have sworn I did."

The giggles were briefly smothered into choking noises, then resurfaced with fresh delight.

"Perhaps," Maggie sang out, spying one sneakered foot peeping out from the foliage, and making as if to creep in the opposite direction, "he went this way, or else—" Without warning, she spun back and flung aside the branches of his hiding spot. "Aha! Just as I thought, my little Munchkin!"

Squealing with glee, he huddled away from her as she stalked him farther into his little cave. And then, too late, she heard the growl, too late saw the black shape rise threateningly from the cool green shadows and launch itself toward her.

CHAPTER THREE

INSTINCTIVELY, Maggie froze, curling herself into a tight ball with her arms wrapped protectively around her head, and waited for the attack. When it came, it was not exactly the vicious tearing of flesh that her overactive imagination had anticipated. It was, however, violent, like the language that accompanied it. Whether by accident or design, the hand that closed over her hunched shoulders grasped strands of her hair, too, and yanked on them with so little mercy that tears spurted from her eyes.

"You might well cry!" Bennet Montgomery's outraged roar informed her. "Of all the damnfool, idiotic, *suicidal* stunts! Where are your brains, woman, or is it expecting too much that you possess any?"

"I'm not...it didn't—oh, ouch!" Aware that he had dragged her out from under the willow tree in much the same manner as he might haul a sack of potatoes, Maggie made a concerted effort to recoup her dignity.

It was useless. Grass burns scorched her bare legs and stained the full cotton skirt which normally hung to midcalf, but which now was hitched halfway up her thighs. "Will you let me go?" she gasped.

He glared at her, as if it were her fault his damned dog was so vigilant. "Would you mind telling me what on earth possessed you to do such a foolish thing?" he inquired coldly, releasing her so suddenly that she sagged in a heap at his feet.

The injustice of his question restored Maggie faster than any amount of sympathy. "I was doing what you hired me to do," she snapped, "but if that includes having to run foul of your beast, then I think you should be paying me danger money over and above my regular salary."

"Beau is the most civilized animal in the world, and highly intelligent."

"Really?" She inspected her sore knees. Only her first day in this place, and she was beginning to feel— and look—as if she'd just emerged from a battle zone. "You could have fooled me. He reacted as if I were about to inflict bodily harm on Christopher."

"That's because you acted as if you were."

"What?" She stared at him incredulously. "I most certainly did not. We were playing hide-and-seek."

"My dear Miss Jones," Bennet said with a malicious little smile, "I saw you from the patio, pouncing on all fours like an elegant and rather determined cat going after a mouse. Do you really expect any self-respecting guard dog to stand for that kind of behavior from a stranger toward one of its own?"

He delivered his words the way a swordsman might flick a rapier, delicately and so swiftly it would have been hard to believe he'd struck at all, were it not for the bloodstain he left behind.

Indignation tinted her cheeks scarlet. He'd been spying on her! "I would appreciate it, Mr. Montgomery, if, in future, you would keep that dog confined when I am here. I do not intend to have to fight him off every time I come near Christopher."

"Before you go any further in your role as teacher," he replied calmly, extending a hand to help her to her feet, "you're going to spend a little time as a student and learn the proper way to deal with Beau—starting now, so that such measures aren't necessary."

"I'd really prefer not to do that."

"I dare say, Miss Jones." His hand beneath her elbow was peremptory, his tone commanding. "However, I'm not allowing you that option. Beauregarde!"

The dog, which had stationed itself protectively between her and the child, trotted forward and came to a halt far too close to Maggie's leg for her comfort or peace of mind.

"Don't be afraid," Bennet said, as if such a choice were hers to make.

How did she explain to him the reasons for her fear without resurrecting all those parts of her past she was trying so hard to forget? "I can't help it."

"I promise you, he will not hurt you." He spoke with reassuring certainty, but it was the caressing touch of his hand around her wrist, as different from his earlier rough treatment as a kiss from a slap, that persuaded her to trust him. When he sensed that she'd grown less agitated, he slid his fingers down to interlace over the backs of hers. "You are going to hold out your hand and let him sniff it, just like this, see?"

Mesmerised, Maggie watched him draw her arm forward until her palm was within snapping distance of the large mouth.

"And now that he has your scent," Bennet continued, his voice hypnotically low, "you are going to stroke his head, like this. Doesn't he have beautiful fur, Miss Jones? As silky as your hair, I'd say—no, don't stop! You can see from his expression how much he's enjoying that. What man wouldn't?"

She wasn't sure which disturbed her more, Bennet's question or the dog's inquiring nose, which was investigating her knees. One thing, however, was certain—even she could tell the animal's behavior was not aggressive. The realization made her brave. "Nice dog," she said, and dared to fondle his ears.

She immediately wished she hadn't bothered. Beau's response was to rear up on his hind legs, tail thrashing. She backed away. "Oh! Please don't! Sit!" she begged, trying to fend him off, to absolutely no avail.

"*No!*" Bennet spoke sharply, subduing both her and the dog with his command.

"What's wrong?" She looked up at her mentor, disappointed as well as annoyed that he didn't appreciate the courage it had taken for her to get this far.

"*Never* speak to him in that tentative tone of voice. He won't believe you mean a word of what you say."

"Why not? I thought you said he was intelligent."

"So am I, Maggie." Bennet's smile washed over her with sudden, lingering pleasure. "But if I were to take you in my arms and kiss you, and you were to beg me to stop the way you just did with Beau, I would take your words to mean that I could have my way with you—with your blessing."

Without leave, a tiny flame sparked to life somewhere just below her heart. "You would be mistaken," she whispered.

He reached forward to gather up a handful of hair, then let it spill softly through his fingers. "Would I?" he murmured.

She could have pulled away. She should have pulled away. His hand was not detaining her. But his eyes, half-hidden by the long, dark lashes, were. They had fastened on her mouth with quiet possession and she was helpless to retreat. "Mr. Montgomery..." she faltered.

"Be firm, Miss Jones." He coiled her hair around his palm again and brought it to rest against the curve of her neck. "Make your wishes known."

"Let me go," she begged, and quailed at the expression that flared to life in his gaze, dilating the pupils and reducing the irises to smoky gray haloes. Not once, in all the years she'd been married to Eric, had her husband looked at her like that, with such rampant desire.

Then, as though he realized that, in demanding access to her secrets, he was exposing too many of his own, Bennet's gaze softened and he released her. "Perhaps I'm expecting too much, too soon," he said enigmatically. "Come back to the house with me, Miss Jones, and let me pour you a little brandy or something. You look quite pale."

She *felt* pale, as though all the blood had rushed to the core of her, to nourish and support the tiny flame he had fanned into life. She ran the tip of her tongue over her dry lips and looked to where the child amused himself trying to outwit the dog, who refused to allow him to wander too close to the water's edge. "What about Christopher?"

"He's too young for brandy." A brief but disarming grin lightened Bennet's features. "However, I dare say Mrs. Marshall can come up with a suitable alternative and keep him entertained for a while."

"I'm sure she can, but you're paying me to look after him."

"I'm paying you to help him learn to speak properly, which is not something that's likely to happen in one afternoon. Class is over for today."

Still, she hesitated. "I hate to disappoint him. He said he wanted to play hide-and-seek."

"Really?" Bennet raised doubtful brows. "If that's so, then you're to be congratulated. You've made remarkable headway in a very short time."

Christopher, tiring of his game, chose that moment to join them, one hand wrapped around Beau's leather collar. "Herg," he said.

Maggie turned back to Bennet. "Does that convince you?" she asked. "You heard him yourself. 'Hide,' he said."

Bennet's mouth twitched uncontrollably, his amusement this time too dangerously male to qualify as disarming. "I'm afraid you're mistaken, Miss Jones," he purred. "He didn't mean 'hide' at all, he meant 'dog.' And you, in your ignorance, ventured into the jaws of danger, as it were. Not a smart move for a woman as afraid of dogs as you appear to be.''

"I obviously have a great deal still to learn," Maggie observed wryly. "Do you suppose that, in future, Beau will allow me to do so without baring his teeth at me?"

Bennet cupped a proprietorial hand under her elbow and steered her toward the house. "Now that he's been formally introduced, you'll have no more problems. As far as he's concerned, you've just become one of the family."

Ahead of them, Christopher trotted along beside Beau, nattering amiably away in his own private language, barely comprehensible to Maggie's unpracticed ear. "It's rather touching, isn't it, the bond between the two of them?" she said quietly.

Bennet watched as the housekeeper appeared and took the child into the house, then switched his attention to her. "Yes, it is, but right now I find my interest captured more by you. You face twenty or more children every working day, so you're obviously a woman of courage. How did it happen that you're so afraid of dogs?"

It was the sort of question Maggie dreaded, because there was no simple answer. Instead of trying to explain, she merely shrugged. "These things happen sometimes," she answered vaguely.

"Not without reason, they don't," Bennet objected. "Were you bitten when you were a child?"

"No." She stared impassively ahead, aware that he was watching her closely.

"Hmm." He ushered her across the patio and through the double glass doors into a graciously appointed room she hadn't seen before. "Sit down, Miss Jones. Sherry or brandy?"

"Sherry, please." She chose one end of a silk-covered couch, and looked around. "What a lovely room. Did you furnish it yourself?"

If she had hoped to divert his curiosity, she soon learned she'd failed. "I don't want to talk about me," he replied bluntly. "You're the one I'm interested in learning more about."

"My life story's pretty dull."

"Yesterday, I might have accepted that reply. But then I discovered that you live in a tiny house supplied by the school board, either to offset the miserable salary they pay you or because this town is so remote that the inducement of free housing is necessary to persuade staff to move here. And then I find that you've filled the place with artwork that's worth a small fortune, and that your furniture would look more at home in a Manhattan penthouse." He served her sherry in a cut-crystal glass. "And none of that adds up to what I'd call 'dull.'"

"Perhaps I inherited everything," she said, seizing on the half-truth with relief. "It has been known to happen."

"Why don't I quite believe you?"

"I don't know," she sighed, exasperated at his persistence, "but I'm confident you're about to tell me."

Once again, he shook with the sudden laughter that always surprised her and undermined her determination to remain aloof.

"What was it you said yesterday? Something about not being treated like an upstairs maid, because you prefer to give orders rather than take them?" His eyes gleamed with humor. "In light of what I now know, I believe you meant every word, and I have to tell you that, in any other woman, Miss Jones, I'd find such an attitude unacceptable. Yet, for some reason, in you it intrigues me. Why is that, I wonder?"

"You ask far too many questions," she scolded, shifting uneasily on the couch.

"And pry into matters that are none of my business," he concluded for her with a marked lack of regret. "But since we're going to be spending a lot of time together over the next few weeks, it's only natural, surely, to want to learn more about you?" He ran a finger idly along a stack of CDs on a shelf next to the drinks cabinet. "For example, what sort of music do you enjoy—apart from 'Chopsticks'?"

He had a nerve, expecting to ferret out all her secrets, when he'd made it plain enough that his were not for sharing! Still, Maggie wished he weren't so charming under all that male arrogance. And if that was asking for too much, then she heartily wished she found herself better able to resist him. "I doubt we share the same tastes," she said.

"We share more in common than you're willing to admit," he replied quietly, and something—perhaps the way he spoke, or perhaps the glance that accompanied his words—stole past her defenses, causing the flame to gather strength and send warmth flickering along her nerve endings like tiny lightning bolts.

"Really?" She tried not to sound as breathless as she felt, tried to borrow a little of the savoir faire he possessed in such abundance. "Like what?"

He poured himself whisky with a splash of water and came to sit at the opposite end of the couch. "Well, we're both tired of big cities, and we're both looking for a quiet life. We share an interest in Christopher. We're both opinionated and strong-willed. We're both lonely, and—" he shot her a glance from beneath lowered brows "—there's a powerful attraction between us. If it weren't for the fact that I'm not in the least interested in getting involved in a relationship, I'd go so far as to say we might have been made for each other."

Maggie nearly choked on her sherry. "Mr. Montgomery," she retorted in a strangled voice, "your lack of perception is exceeded only by your colossal ego. I am neither lonely nor opinionated, and I am most assuredly not attracted to you, so please don't lose sleep over the notion that I might try to lasso you into a 'relationship' that you're not ready for. Nothing could be further from my mind."

Then she dared to look at him, and saw, too late, that he was teasing her. Sort of.

"Whatever you say, Miss Jones," he murmured placatingly. "Would you care for more sherry?"

With a decisive little clink, she placed her glass on the table beside her. "No, thank you. If I'm to be of any use at all to Christopher, I'll have to do some preparation, which will involve a fair amount of textbook research, and the sooner I get started the better. He's not exactly your everyday four-year-old." Any more than Bennet Montgomery was your everyday guardian!

Bennet expelled a sigh. "What a relief! I was afraid I'd really put my foot in it just now, and that you'd changed your mind about taking the job."

"The idea did occur to me," she informed him, "but that would have been punishing the child for the sins of the uncle, don't you think? Hardly a very professional attitude, I'd say."

"Hardly." He smiled, all agreeable charm now that he'd gotten what he'd wanted from the beginning. "However, before you bury yourself in textbook theories, why don't you resign yourself to staying past regular working hours, just this once, and let me tell you everything I learned from Christopher's speech therapist? I think you'll find it time well spent. In fact, I'd go so far as to say the information is vital if the continuity of my nephew's progress is to be maintained."

He was right, of course, and she was wrong to let the fact annoy her. Textbooks didn't hold the answers for a child like Chris. "Very well," she conceded.

"Excellent!" Springing up from the couch, Bennet headed for the door. "I'll let Mrs. Marshall know there'll be one more for dinner, then we'll get started."

"Just a minute!" Maggie's annoyance bubbled over once more. "I agreed to stay late so that we could work, not so that we could share a cozy dinner for two."

"For three," he corrected her. "And we still have to eat, don't we?"

"Not together," she said primly. "We can eat later, and separately. I meant what I said this morning, Mr. Montgomery. I intend that our association be kept strictly professional."

"You're really hung up on that word 'professional,' Miss Jones," he grumbled. "What are you afraid of? That if we share a simple meal, I might forget myself and take a bite out of you?"

His ability to unravel her composure with his outrageous suggestions both amazed and disconcerted Maggie, partly because he could be forbiddingly distant when he chose, but more because she had no idea she'd be so susceptible to the covertly seductive images his words conjured up. "The only thing I'm afraid of," she snapped, fishing in her bag for a pen, "is that, unless we stop sparring and get down to work, I'll accomplish very little with your nephew and he'll never be ready for kindergarten in September. Do you have some paper I can use to make notes?"

He smiled gently, as though he knew exactly what it was that had her so rattled, and hunted through a drawer in the table beside him. "I'm sure I have, somewhere...ah, yes! How about this?" He held up the sort of notepad a musician might use to write down a musical score.

"It'll do." She paused while he resettled himself on the couch. "Now, what sort of things did the speech therapist recommend for Christopher?"

"One of the most important things," Bennet began, folding his arms behind his head and staring reflectively at the ceiling, "is to make him look at you when you speak to him. Specifically, Miss Jones, he must watch your mouth, and you must exaggerate enunciation of those sounds that give him difficulty."

She nodded, scribbling busily. "Like *D*s."

"Precisely. You would open your mouth wide to say 'dog,' for instance, then get him to imitate you. He has to overcome the habit of speaking nasally."

"Especially with hard consonants, I imagine."

"Right. With *T*, for example, as in the word 't-e-a.'" He swung his gaze to her and stretched his lips wide, emphasizing the facial movement. "Let me see you do it."

"T-e-a," she repeated, trying not to feel self-conscious.

"Very good. What pretty teeth you have, Miss Jones."

The blood rushed to her face once again. "Now look, Mr—"

"'T-e-e-th.' See the difference the extra letters make?"

How could she not, with the tip of his tongue peeking out at her like that? And when was she going to stop letting him goad her into making an idiot of herself?

"The thing to avoid," he went on blithely, "is correcting him all the time. Occasionally, of course, you must, and some days will be worse than others. As you've already seen, when his usual routine is upset, he tends to regress rather badly, but once he learns to trust you and settles down you'll find he's very eager to please."

"Are you saying I should overlook his mistakes? Reinforcing bad habits generally isn't a good idea, you know."

Bennet seemed to find her starchy response vastly entertaining. "Tell me, Miss Jones, do you work on your schoolmarm image by tying up your hair in a tight little knot on the top of your head, perching granny glasses on the end of your nose, and wearing dowdy clothes when you stand before a class?"

"I don't need to, Mr. Montgomery," she retorted. "I'm quite effective enough the way I look now."

He grinned cheerfully. "At last we agree on something!"

She pursed her lips and sat with pen poised, not deigning to enter further into a verbal battle she'd very likely lose. "What else should I know?"

"Well, when he doesn't say a word properly, simply repeat it correctly, then go on with whatever you're doing."

"You make it all sound very simple."

He shrugged. "It is, and it isn't. You really have two jobs. First, you have to undo old, bad habits which, as you no doubt realize, is always a bit of a trial. Then you have to instill the right way of doing things. That means, on top of clear enunciation, you must also encourage him to speak in full sentences.''

"I'm not sure I understand what you mean."

"You would if you'd spent more time with him. He tends to get by with one word sometimes, and two or three at the most."

"I see. You mean, the way a baby does—'cookie,' 'milk,' that sort of thing?"

Bennet nodded. "Or 'dog,'" he reminded her, his smile bewitching her anew. "He also uses his hands a great deal to try to express himself. Both habits are a direct result of having seen his mother use sign language. He even uses a few signs himself. The problem is that although he understands, for example, what the word 'bird' means, both in sign and spoken language, he has no understanding at all that crows, eagles and robins are all birds. He communicates in a very unsophisticated way, you see."

Maggie was afraid she did, and began to wonder if she was equal to the task she'd taken on. "What else?" she asked, rather faintly.

"Prepositions," Bennet declared, as if they were the most riveting subject in the world for the average four-year-old.

"Mr. Montgomery," she unthinkingly protested. "I don't teach prepositions even to my normal students."

His geniality disappeared like a light going out in a windowless room. "Miss Jones," he replied cuttingly, "I do hope you will refrain from using words like 'normal' in front of my nephew. He's quite aware enough that he's different from other children his age without your rubbing it in.''

His rebuke was a slap in the face which she richly deserved, a subduing reminder that her primary focus was the child in need of help and not the uncle whose pervasive charm she found so tempting. ''It's a little late for me to apologize,'' she said, ''but I hope you believe me when I say that you're not nearly as offended by my carelessness as I am. I should, and do, know better. I'm afraid I was caught off guard by your remark, but it won't happen again.''

''Unfortunately,'' Bennet said, his manner softening somewhat, ''it might. The pitfalls involved in what you're about to undertake aren't always the most obvious. Helping Chris overcome his speech difficulties is a physical goal, something that can be measured in tangibles—certain words today, complete sentences next week—but resurrecting his sense of personal worth is too elusive an achievement to be so simply gauged.'' Bennet spread his hands, and sighed heavily. ''Sometimes I wonder if he'll ever regain the sort of confidence that ought to be every child's birthright.''

''Is his life really so terribly unhappy?''

''His mother is dead and his father has rejected him. Isn't that enough?''

''More than enough,'' she replied, ''but at least he's not entirely alone in the world. He does have you.''

Something close to self-contempt flickered in Bennet's eyes. ''Dealing with other people and determining their needs isn't my forte, Miss Jones. I try not to let it show, but the plain fact of the matter is I'd rather face a pack of wild animals any day. At least I know where I stand with them."

Maggie might have believed him if she hadn't seen for herself how sensitively he'd managed to reach inside Christopher's isolation and draw the boy out. But, for reasons he chose not to disclose, he wanted her to believe otherwise. It was just as well. Already, she was too intrigued by him. "Nevertheless, you elected to take on responsibility for a four-year-old," she remarked dispassionately, "and I find that admirable."

"You don't know me well enough to find me admirable or despicable," he informed her, his tone curt. "I suggest you stick to evaluating your student, whom you're somewhat better qualified to judge."

Don't be rude, she was tempted to retort, and would have done so without hesitation if he'd been one of her students. But Bennet Montgomery was not a child, he was a man, and so accustomed to being firmly in control of himself and everything around him that the only way she was going to be able to work effectively with the child was by adopting a nonconfrontational attitude with the uncle whenever possible.

"Tell me more about these prepositions, Mr. Montgomery," she invited softly. "I'm sure you're not really suggesting I introduce Christopher to advanced grammar at his tender age."

Bennet sighed again and rose from the couch, flexing his shoulders in relaxing circles to ease the tension of cramped muscles. "It's almost sunset," he said, crossing to the window and staring out. "Stay and have dinner with us, please, Miss Jones. Think of it as a business invitation if it makes you feel better, because I'm sure that you'll learn far more by observing Christopher for an hour in a situation with which he's familiar and comfortable than I can tell you in six. Then, once Mrs. Marshall's taken him off for his bath, we can discuss any further questions that might arise, and I promise to have you home before nine-thirty."

What was it about single fathers? Maggie wondered, shaking her head at herself for weakening so easily. Technically, Bennet might be only Christopher's guardian, but there was such a wealth of love in his voice when he talked about the child that, whether he was ready to acknowledge it or not, he might as well have been the true parent. And whether he knew it or not, he wielded formidable power with that love. Some women might be able to resist it, but she wasn't one of them. "Thank you for giving me the chance to change my mind," she said. "If I can have a few minutes to tidy myself up, I'd like very much to stay."

He swung back to face her, then, and his smile was neither arrogant nor triumphant but so sincerely sweet that it almost bowled her over. "What a lovely, gracious lady you are, Maggie Jones," he murmured, "and how lucky we are to have found you."

CHAPTER FOUR

THE dinner was like no other Maggie had experienced before, an occasion of understated elegance and wonderful food, both of which were outstripped by the company. She'd grown used to luxury during her marriage, had acquired a taste for exotic foods, and learnt to discriminate between one vintage wine and another. Sterling and Baccarat were commonplace in the Carlson-Lewis household, as was china flamboyantly stamped in gold with the family crest.

Bennet's table was less ostentatious, but there was no mistaking the quality of the heavy silver or the classic perfection of the Steuben crystal. And while poached salmon, tiny new potatoes drowning in butter and parsley, and tossed green salad might rate as ordinary to more elevated palates, Maggie found the simple meal superb. But it was the atmosphere that struck her most forcibly, the charm of recorded harpsichord music playing softly in the background and the warmth of genuine love and laughter between Bennet and Christopher.

On his best behavior, the child was a joy. It was as if, to compensate for all the obstacles he'd had to face in other areas of his life, God had endowed him with a special sort of beauty and more than his share of social graces. His manners were outstanding. When he appeared in the dining room, his pale blond hair shiningly neat, he waited until Bennet had seated Maggie before scrambling onto his own chair. He knew exactly which fork to use, and was painstakingly careful to eat with his mouth closed—major accomplishments in so young a child, as Maggie was only too aware.

He seemed to find her presence fascinating, and fixed his vivid blue eyes on her for long moments at a time. At last, after he'd given her a particularly close and lengthy scrutiny as she sipped her wine, his uncle protested.

"It's rude to stare, Christopher," he observed, "even when a lady as pretty as Miss Jones stays for dinner." But his reproach was mildly offered and undermined with amusement.

Christopher's Botticelli-angel face broke into a shy smile. "Pretty," he slurred, before his gaze drifted from Maggie to his plate.

She wanted to hug him—and his uncle—and wished she was more deserving of the compliment. The crisp cotton shirtwaister had wilted over the course of the day, and even at its best would have been inappropriate for the occasion. Bennet had found time to change into a plain white linen shirt and black pants. At the very least, she ought to have been wearing pearls.

As the meal progressed, however, her appearance assumed secondary importance as she witnessed for herself what Bennet had meant when he'd said the child's grasp of sentences was limited to two or three words. "Perhaps Miss Jones would like more salad, Chris," Bennet suggested at one point. "Why don't you ask her?"

For a second, Chris struggled with the word "salad," managing the first syllable well enough, but stumbling over the second, and finally settling simply for, "More?"

"I would love more salad," Maggie replied, enunciating each sound clearly, fully aware that Bennet was taking careful note of her handling of the situation.

"Do you understand now what I was trying to explain?" he asked, once Christopher was upstairs getting ready for bed, and they had returned to the living room for coffee.

"Yes. His speech level is not much more advanced than that of a two-year-old, although his comprehension is, I suspect, higher than average for his age."

"I agree," Bennet replied. "And, as I mentioned earlier, he's very eager to learn. I'm hoping that will motivate him to make great strides in overcoming his difficulties."

"Does he watch television very much?"

"Not really. Why do you ask?"

"Because speech depends on hearing, and he surely needs to be exposed to sound as much as possible."

"True enough," Bennet replied, "but consider for a moment the sort of shows geared for the average four-year-old: clowns, animated puppets, cartoons, things like that."

She nodded. "Puppets in particular. They're a wonderful teaching tool."

"But not for Chris."

Oh, surely Bennet wasn't one of those purists who thought children should never be exposed to anything less than the classics? Didn't he know that variety was the spice that made young minds curious to learn more? "Why ever not?"

"Think about it. Puppets, or people dressed up, say, as birds with beaks, don't open and close their mouths the way we do. Also, their speech is usually distorted, to fit the role. Chris can't learn by watching them, and he shouldn't be trying to imitate them. Sounding like Donald Duck isn't what we're trying to teach him."

The reasons were so obvious and logical that Maggie was ashamed not to have thought of them for herself. However, they didn't provide the answer to her original question. "Then who does he listen to, apart from you and Mrs. Marshall?"

"What makes you assume he needs anyone else?"

"Mr. Montgomery," Maggie protested, "doesn't it occur to you that the reason he reacts so poorly around other people is that he's never exposed to anything other than just the two of you—not even to the artificial world of television?"

Her observations seemed to unsettle Bennet completely. He got up from the couch and paced restlessly back and forth in front of the fireplace, as though the living room were too confining suddenly. "I can't imagine him being able to resist you for more than a day at the most, Miss Jones, if that's what's worrying you."

She recognized immediately that his answer was a calculated attempt to flatter and distract her, and she was afraid she knew why. Taking up her notepad again, she shook her head at his silent offer of brandy, and waited pointedly until he'd poured an inch for himself. It was time to speak her mind bluntly and she wanted his full attention before she replied. "Let's not pretend I was fishing for compliments, Mr. Montgomery. You've as good as admitted that Christopher's interpersonal skills are severely hampered by the isolation imposed on him during his early years, yet it's a situation you're fostering by keeping him locked up here."

"Good Lord, Miss Jones, he's hardly a prisoner!" Bennet burst out, clearly affronted by her suggestion.

"I didn't mean to imply that he was," Maggie returned evenly, "but you must be aware that, even if we manage to bring his speech skills up to par, there is another problem that isn't going to be resolved until you agree to make a few changes in his daily routines."

Bennet stopped pacing to fiddle with the wicks of the candles on the mantelpiece, then touched a match to them. They gave off just enough light to offset the gloom of dusk and allow Maggie to take further notes if she wished. "What are you getting at, Miss Jones?"

There was no point in trying to be subtle. "You can't fling him into a classroom full of exuberant four to six-year-olds in a few weeks' time, and expect him to survive without any previous experiences at relating to other children."

"Nonsense!" Bennet scoffed. "That's the same as saying that an only child is handicapped because he has no brothers or sisters."

"No, it's not. Norm—" Hastily, she bit back the word. "As a rule, an only child has friends."

"Christopher has friends," he argued defensively.

"Not his own age, he doesn't. His friends are adult, extremely limited, and selected not to damage his already fragile ego. I like children, especially four to six-year-olds, Mr. Montgomery, which is why I chose a career as a primary schoolteacher. But I'm the first to admit that they can be little savages when they choose. Give them a victim and they'll more often than not make his life miserable."

"A good teacher," Bennet remarked stiffly, "can surely put a stop to that kind of thing before it takes hold."

"I'm a very good teacher, but I don't plan to hold your nephew's hand every minute he's under my care." She saw the stubborn set of his jaw and stifled a sigh. Hadn't she suspected from the very beginning that he'd be one of those difficult parents? "Look, the point I'm trying to make is that once he's comfortable with me I think you have to allow me to start taking him out regularly—to the park, say, or to the store—so that he has the chance to spend time around other children of his age before he finds himself confined with them in a classroom all day."

"Absolutely not! I told you at the outset that I will not have him paraded in front of the whole town, not until—"

That did it! Maggie had heard enough of this nonsense. "And I'm telling you that your pride is going to have to take a back seat to that child's welfare, unless you want him to become hopelessly neurotic!" she shot back heatedly. "*I* use the word 'normal' without any insult intended, and you go off the deep end with a big splash, accusing me of discriminating against him. But it strikes me that *you*'re the one who's treating him differently. I think you want to keep him hidden until he's as *normal* as every other child in town, which might take a very long time. The question is, why? Can it be that you're ashamed of him the way he is now?"

Bennet's face remained impassive, but his eyes smoldered. "Are you a trained psychologist all of a sudden?"

"No, but I'm perfectly willing to consult one."

"Well, I already did, so don't bother."

"And?"

"And what?"

"What did he say?"

"That's none of your business."

Maggie stared at him, temporarily at a loss for words. The man was worse than difficult, he was impossible! Obviously, the psychologist's opinion coincided with hers, and, just as obviously, Bennet wasn't about to admit it.

He extended his arms along the mantelpiece and glowered at the tiled hearth, his rigid stance a warning in itself. "You're overstepping your authority, Miss Jones," he advised.

Realizing again that confrontation would merely alienate him further, Maggie took a different approach. "Don't you think," she asked softly, going to stand behind him and resting a gentle hand against that unyielding spine, "that, as Christopher's teacher and someone who shares your concern for him, I have a right to know?"

"Don't talk to me about rights," he retorted bitterly, shrugging her off. "I sometimes think I've spent half my life considering other people's rights at the expense of my own."

Unexpectedly, the conversation had swung focus, and it was not Christopher they were discussing at all, but this stranger, who possessed such an uncanny ability to reach past her professional self and touch the private woman so few people really knew anymore. In his own way, Bennet felt as alone and betrayed as the child he'd rescued. It wasn't right or reasonable that she should feel such compulsion to change any of that, she told herself firmly, yet in the next breath heard herself beg, "Tell me what you mean. I'd like to understand."

At that, Bennet turned his head and flung her a look of blistering scorn. "How can you possibly understand? Did you grow up expected to set a perfect example for your younger brother? Were you made to feel responsible for that brother's success or lack of it when, in fact, he had neither a tenth of your talent nor a fraction of the self-discipline required to raise that talent above mediocrity?"

"I have only one older sister, but she—"

"Have you spent most of your life obligated to live up to an image not necessarily of your own making?"

She'd been married to Eric for only a few years, but it had seemed an eternity at the time. "As a matter of fact—"

His hands chopped the air, savage as a guillotine, dismissing her response before it was uttered. "Or been saddled with the burden of being born the fortunate one in the family—?" His mouth, which could mold itself along such tender lines when he looked at Chris, twisted in contempt. "As if luck has anything to do with the sheer hard work and determination it takes to be the best!"

"Well, no, but—"

"Then how on earth can you expect to understand?"

The question lashed her with an anger whose roots went back to a time long before he'd ever known her. Maggie almost felt sorry for Francis, second-best and second-born to such a paragon, but decided not to say so. It would be safer to agree that Bennet was right, that she couldn't possibly know how he felt, and thereby distance herself from him. Already, after only a day, she found him so disturbingly attractive that, whenever he looked at her or came close enough to touch her, alarm bells went off inside. But, for all that he tried not to let it show, he was a man in pain, and that made turning her back on him impossible. It simply wasn't in her nature, anymore than it was to prevaricate.

"You're not just angry with your brother because of the way he treated his wife and child," she declared, comprehension dawning. "You've resented him all your life."

"Well, don't sound so surprised, Miss Jones," Bennet returned, with blistering sarcasm. "I'm not the first to suffer from sibling rivalry. Read the Old Testament if you don't believe me. There've been times in the past when I could really relate to how Cain felt."

"But you worked closely with your brother for years. How could you stand it, feeling as you do?"

"Because when I'm not busy hating Francis for the messes he continues to make of his life, and which I invariably have to clean up, I'm as susceptible to his charm as anyone else. I suppose I love him. Unfortunately, I cannot respect him." He raised his shoulders, a touch of bitter humor seasoning his anger. "He's Peter Pan in the flesh, Boy Wonder who never grew up."

"I know what you mean," she felt compelled to say, even though her words might provoke his further scorn. "I met him once."

"You?" He looked astonished.

She waved a hand dismissingly. The time to talk about her years as Eric's wife was not now, if ever. "Oh, it was just for a moment, after a concert."

"I thought you weren't a fan of classical music."

"I'm not." She laughed. "I was sort of dragged there against my will—but I enjoyed it anyway."

"Are you telling me we met *before* yesterday?"

"No. I was introduced only to your brother."

His mouth curled disdainfully. "And you were dazzled."

"I found him," she said, treading a fine line between honesty and discretion, "exactly as you just described him—a thoroughly charming Peter Pan."

Bennet laced his fingers and flexed them gently, a little smile on his lips, but his eyes, she noticed, were unamused. "No wonder you didn't notice me," he said.

"Why would I?" she answered rashly, intolerably moved by his loneliness. "You were already a man, and I was too young and inexperienced to appreciate that fact. But Francis? Bennet, you and I both know he'll always be a boy."

He came to stand close to her then, without actually touching her. She could feel the heat of his body, and almost trembled from the electricity that seemed to emanate from him. His height and breadth blocked out the dying light from the garden, and all she could see of him was what the gleam of the candles chose to reveal: his dark hair and the aristocratic planes of his face.

"Will you believe me when I tell you that not once in all the years since I became a man have I met a woman quite like you?" he murmured. "How lucky Christopher is to know you before life strips him of his ideals."

He lifted his hand and dipped a finger under the gold chain that hung around her neck, pulling her forward that extra fraction of an inch until they were

one breathless millisecond away from a kiss. And
Maggie found herself believing what he'd said. He
could have convinced her of anything at that moment, with the sun gone down and crickets chirping
outside, and candlelight playing tag in his eyes.

But only for an instant. She'd made rules and,
teacher that she was, she believed they were there for
a purpose and should be followed. She hardly knew
him, yet she was acting as much like a fool as she had
the night she'd met his brother, willing to suspend reality for a fleeting moment of improbability. The difference was, she was a lot older now and ought to
know better. "Mr. Montgomery," she reproved him,
quaveringly to be sure, but it was enough to break the
spell.

"Yes, Miss Jones." He straightened to his full
height and stepped away, that mask of proud reserve
she was beginning to recognize cloaking the tenderness that had almost betrayed him a moment earlier.
"Back to business, right?"

"Right," she echoed with faint enthusiasm. Sometimes it would be nice not to be so damned inflexible
with oneself. And it would be wonderful to be un-
touched by those failures of yesterday that made her
afraid to take chances today. "We were discussing—"
what *had* they been talking about, before they'd got
sidetracked by personal issues? "—your rights as
Christopher's uncle versus mine as his teacher."

"I prefer to think of it as your rights as my employee versus mine as the man who pays your salary."

They were back to business with a vengeance! "If money were my chief priority, Mr. Montgomery," she flared, "I'd be earning a living at something more lucrative than teaching. You're familiar with the word 'vocation,' I'm sure, so please don't insult me by suggesting I'd exchange my professional integrity for dollars."

"A praiseworthy attitude, I'm sure," he remarked cuttingly, "but your timing's all wrong. If I'd met you ten years ago, I might have been swayed, but as things now stand I'm too hardened a case to believe in you."

She'd regret it later, she knew, but she couldn't help herself. "And I don't believe you," she said. "You almost kissed me a moment ago, and I almost let you, not for any of the reasons these things usually happen—I learned long ago not to be deceived by superficialities—but because I was touched by the tenderness and sweetness that you work so hard to keep hidden."

"Don't delude yourself," he almost sneered. "You're looking at a man whose best friend is a dog, Miss Jones, and do you know why? Because in the whole world, Beau is the only one who lets me be myself and still offers me unqualified devotion, approval and loyalty. 'Tenderness and sweetness' aren't exactly my strong points."

"Are you saying, then, that you're just putting up with Christopher? That there's no love or commitment between the two of you?"

He closed his eyes wearily. "Go home, Miss Jones, and spare me your amateur analysis. It's past your bedtime. Or must I practically kiss you again to get rid of you?''

Snatching up her bag, Maggie rose to her feet, stung. She was a bigger fool than even she'd thought. ''That won't be necessary.''

''Praise the Lord!''

''But I won't back off about Chris. He's not going to end up a hermit like you.''

''Oh, leave me alone! And leave Chris out of this.''

''No! It might be too late for you, but that child deserves to live a full and happy life and, now that I'm officially in charge of him, I intend to see he gets it.''

''Don't push me too far,'' he cautioned her.

''Ha!'' Maggie glared at him defiantly as she swept out of the room and down the hall, aware that, as a rebuttal, her response had fallen a long way short of scintillating.

Bennet realized it, too. She saw the smile that suddenly turned up the corners of his mouth despite his struggle to prevent it, which only served to make her annoyance all the more intense. Because the bottom line, as they both knew, was that he was the boss and would have the last word.

As he strode past her to fling open the front door, his thigh whispered against her hip. A brief contact, to be sure, but electrifying enough to remind her that, no matter how prickly an adversary or misguided an uncle Bennet Montgomery might be, he was, more than anything else, a man she found impossible to ignore.

And he knew it! That mercurial gleam of humor in his eyes had given him away again. She swept past him, clinging to her dignity by a thread. "Good evening, Mr. Montgomery."

His voice floated after her, a beguiling baritone. "Good evening, Maggie. Watch your step."

It wasn't her step she was worried about. It was her emotional well-being. He threatened it. He was altogether too intuitive—and, worse, he was forthright. She wasn't used to that in a man.

Eric had perfected the art of innuendo. The only time he'd stated his feelings clearly and unequivocally was the day she had filed for divorce. "Sue me for mental cruelty, you little bitch," he'd threatened, "and I'll give new meaning to the term, the scope of which not even you could begin to imagine. No one drags my name through the mud, least of all a mousy little schoolteacher from Canada who didn't know the difference between gingerale and champagne until she married me."

Ludicrous that she should be more afraid of Bennet Montgomery now than she'd been of Eric then. Ludicrous, too, the notion that, of the two men, Bennet was much more dangerous. Yet her heart was tripping and stalling like an overwound clock, and the crevices of her palms were damp where her nails had dug into them.

In little more than twenty-four hours Bennet had given her a storehouse of special moments, studded with little gems of tenderness and nuances of passion. And, in doing so, he'd made her regret the things that were missing from her life, instead of making her thankful for what she had.

She ought to turn down the job and stay as far away from him as possible. But she wouldn't. Not because of Christopher—Bennet obviously had the means to import the best therapist in the province if she refused him—but because she couldn't, even though the common sense she'd bragged about yesterday warned her that, like the proverbial moth, she was irresistibly drawn to a flame that might very well consume her. And the name of that flame was Bennet Montgomery.

CHAPTER FIVE

THE next several weeks were, in some ways, the most rewarding in Maggie's professional experience. Once his initial shyness subsided, Chris blossomed and, if all his difficulties didn't magically disappear, at least he overcame enough of them so that his progress was significant and his improvement obvious to the most untrained observer.

"Amazing!" Mrs. Marshall confided, on one occasion. "He almost speaks English now!"

Not the sort of remark that would have endeared her to Bennet, had he overheard, perhaps, but Maggie accepted it in the spirit in which it was intended—as a compliment, pure and simple. The boy who couldn't say "dog" at the beginning of July, was asking to "play with Beau" by the month's end, and, if the *B* sometimes got lost, the meaning was clear enough.

Unfortunately, Maggie's personal life was less than satisfactory, and she had Bennet to thank for that. His behavior left her utterly confused. It was as though he was a man at war with himself, who blamed and resented her for disturbing his peace—except for those times when he appeared to take nothing but pleasure in her company. Yet Maggie knew that to confront him about his contradictory attitude would entail only embarrassment, since he never did anything overt to which a reasonable person could take exception.

The thing that unsettled her most was his habit of watching her when she was working with Chris, though he seldom chose to join them in their games. Often, the only warning she'd have that he was near by would be in the sudden alertness that stole over Beau. The dog would grow very still, ears pricked and tail on the brink of waving, and Maggie would turn to discover Bennet standing at one of the open windows or in the shade of a nearby tree.

When he realized he'd been spotted, he'd disappear as hastily as if he'd been caught spying, an accusation she was reluctant to make, since she knew that, if she gave him such an opening, he'd almost certainly denounce her as paranoid. She might almost have been convinced that his vigilance arose because he neither liked nor trusted her, except that, sometimes, she encountered an expression of warmth in his eyes too closely laced with desire for it to have been meant for Christopher.

And then there were those other, less frequent times when Bennet would deliberately seek her out alone, perhaps when the boy was napping or after classes were over. One day in particular stood out as memorable because it marked new heights of awareness in their reactions to each other.

Shortly before Maggie had finished work it had started to rain, not very heavily, just enough to settle the summer dust and fill the air with the scent of flowers. It was the sort of rare afternoon people in the high country treasured, a respite from the baking, almost desertlike heat, and Maggie hadn't minded that she'd have to walk home. In fact, she'd looked forward to the feel of the warm rain misting her hair and face.

But Bennet had caught her just as she was setting out. "Wait until it stops," he said, sliding his hand down her arm to circle her waist. It was the first time he'd touched her in weeks.

"It won't last long, it's only a shower," she replied, her gaze drawn to the long, strong fingers that were far too sensitive not to have felt the sudden leap of her pulse at his touch.

"Then it won't make much difference to your plans for later on if you wait until it's over," he said, drawing her into the music room. "Would you care for something? Iced tea, maybe, or lemonade?"

Like a ninny, she followed him, despite the sixth sense that told her she'd be better off braving the rain. "All right," she agreed, thinking that a cold drink might snap her out of her trance.

But having made the offer, he promptly forgot to follow up on it. "What do you do when you're finished here for the day, Maggie?" he asked.

"Go home," she replied blankly, wondering where the conversation was leading. She soon found out.

"And stay there," he persisted, "all evening?"

"Usually, yes."

"By yourself?"

"Of course. You know I live alone."

"Well, you might have a . . . friend."

She almost burst out laughing as the real reason for his curiosity became clear. "You mean a man, Mr. Montgomery?"

"I don't see what's so hilarious about that," he snapped, looking discomfited. "What's the matter? Don't you like men?"

"Yes," she said, unable to dispel her smile. "I like men—at least, most men."

He grew very still. "Do you like me?"

His eyes were unreadable, but the devastating honesty in his voice demanded nothing less than absolute truth in her answer. "Yes," she told him soberly. "I do. I like you very much. Far more, I'm afraid, than is wise."

He lifted his hand to her cheek, a whisper of a caress so tender that it took her breath away. "Don't be afraid, Maggie," he murmured, his gaze cherishing her.

Then the sun shot past the clouds and slanted into the room to turn his eyes silver and fracture the moment into brilliant prisms of light. And Bennet reacted like a man rescued on the brink of making a fatal error. He withdrew his hand and stepped away from her. "It's stopped raining," he said with unmistakable relief. "You can go home now, if you wish."

What was she supposed to say? That she'd rather stay? That she wanted him to take her in his arms and kiss her? There was a limit to how truthful she could be, even with herself. "You're right," she said.

Anger fueled her all the way home and throughout a four-mile run around the lake. At the end of it she felt cleansed, but no closer to understanding him. All she knew was that being around him left her feeling like a yo-yo on a string, reeled in one minute and flung away the next. And she didn't like it. Even though she knew he was different and that it was unfair of her, she couldn't help comparing him to Eric. Not that Bennet was cruel or vindictive or cold, but his refusal to confront his own emotions left her feeling too much like the victim in her relationship with him, and that was a role she wouldn't tolerate again.

As a result, resentment began to build inside her and, although she tried to keep it hidden, things came to a head the day he received the invitation.

Every year on the second Saturday in August, John Keyes, the school principal, hosted a barbecue on the beach to which he invited any of his staff members who were in town, in addition to as many parents and other residents as cared to attend. Between eighty and a hundred people usually showed up.

John was a local boy whose father owned one of the big cattle ranches outside Sagepointe, and the barbecue was probably the high point of the summer in town, if only because John Keyes senior supplied a side of beef that tested the resolve of the most dedicated vegetarian. Another farmer provided potatoes and corn on the cob so fresh and sweet that it defied description, and Edith Caverley, whose talent as a gossip monger was exceeded only by her skill in the kitchen, baked cakes. Everyone else brought the rest: salads and pickles, sun-warmed tomatoes just off the vine, cheese and farm fresh cream, peaches drowned in homemade brandy, and tiny wild strawberries.

Everyone had a good time. Howard Stills, who ran the post office, played his banjo; his crony, Walt Murphy, played the harmonica. Mrs. Murphy forgot that she didn't really like Mrs. Stills, and, for that one day only, Edith Caverley forgave John Keyes junior for having given her grandson a *D* in math.

There was a tug-of-war, a singsong around a fire, and someone always got thrown in the lake. It was a day of what John Keyes senior called "plain, old-fashioned horsing-around-good-fun and food." Maggie had loved her initiation last year, and expected to have as good a time this. What she didn't expect was that Bennet would come swooping down on her in the garden, the Tuesday morning before the event, dark brows drawn together in a scowl, and accuse her of getting him involved in a social free-for-all in which he had no wish to partake.

"You know how I feel about these things," he railed at her, the minute Christopher had disappeared inside the house for his midmorning snack with Mrs. Marshall.

"Well, don't yell at me," Maggie flung back. "It wasn't my suggestion to invite you. If you want to know the truth, I, too, would rather you hadn't been asked. I'll have a much better time without you there."

He wasn't particularly pleased with her response. "Well, that's a fine attitude, I must say! What have I ever done to you to deserve something like that?"

What, indeed? Maggie rolled her eyes.

She could count on one hand the minutes they'd spent alone together since that day in the music room. Nevertheless, he was still always *there*, making his presence felt. If he wasn't actually within sight, she could hear him trying out new arrangements in preparation for his next concert tour, which, according to Mrs. Marshall, was scheduled for the autumn.

On top of that, there was lunch every day, a whole hour during which Chris got to show off his accomplishments, and she got to sit there under the surveillance of his uncle's observant gray eyes. Maggie had no doubt that Bennet knew to the last detail which clothes she'd worn on which day, and could probably give accurate inventory of her entire summer wardrobe.

"Look," she said now, reaching up to secure the combs which held back her hair and trying hard to ignore the way his gaze followed the upward sweep of her arm, "it's up to John whom he asks to his party, and he's much too nice a man not to have invited you. But you're not obligated to accept, and you certainly have no right to bellow at me. A simple 'No, thanks' when he phoned would have sufficed."

"That would have been boorish," Bennet muttered, having the grace to appear a little shamefaced, and cast a trapped look around at the flower beds. "But, either way, I refuse to take Christopher along."

Maggie shook her head. "What a pity. He'd probably have a ball."

"And what if he didn't? What if exposure to so many strangers set him back?"

"That's something you're going to have to risk finding out very soon if you expect him to make any sort of transition to a classroom in just over a month." She slanted a glance at him, aware that she was touching on a sore point. "You can't keep him in isolation forever, you know. This might be the perfect opportunity to broaden his horizons a bit before school starts."

Bennet's sigh heralded his irritation. "I know you're the teacher and you're supposed to know everything, but do you always have to be right?"

It seemed to be like this whenever the two of them tried to talk to one another these days, even though they confined their discussions either to Chris or some mutually neutral subject like the weather. They bickered, as though neither one could bear for the other to have the last word on anything. If it weren't that his looks still told her otherwise, she'd have thought that he disliked her intensely. "I'm not always right," she admitted, "but in this particular instance..."

Before she'd taken Chris off for his snack, Mrs. Marshall had brought out a tray with a pot of coffee and two cups. "In this particular instance, you're not wrong," Bennet said wryly. "Is there enough coffee in that pot for me?"

"Of course. That's why there are two cups."

"Well, take a little sugar in yours," he retorted. "You could use the sweetening."

Maggie flushed, knowing the criticism was deserved. It wasn't the first time she'd been snappy with him, but she couldn't seem to help herself. It was her only defense against the inroads he continued to make on her affections. The attraction between them hadn't lessened. It enveloped her like a presence, whether he was in the room with her or not, and what made things worse was the knowledge that it wasn't just something that hinged on runaway hormones. Her emotions were now involved, too, and they frightened her.

She still found Bennet handsome, of course. Whether it was the slower pace of country living that had lessened the signs of strain around his eyes and mouth, or the summer tan he'd so easily acquired, she couldn't decide, but she found him, if anything, even more physically attractive than she had before. But his appearance had meshed with other facets of his personality to create a whole more diverse than good looks alone could ever be.

He was, she knew, a complicated man—talented, solitary, and often at odds with himself. The characteristics he showed to the outside world—the impatience, the arrogance, the reclusiveness—were just a front to cover up a softer side that he seemed almost ashamed to reveal to her. Yet it showed in the way he treated Mrs. Marshall, with an affection and respect that wouldn't have been inappropriate toward an aunt, let alone a housekeeper. And it showed in his treatment of Christopher. He loved the boy as if he were his own son.

In witnessing all this, Maggie had learnt something about herself that she'd rather not have faced. When she'd divorced Eric, she had decided that being alone was far preferable to being trapped in a bad marriage, and that it would take a very long time and a very special man to persuade her to give up her independence a second time. She could lead a perfectly content life with just herself for company, she'd thought. Yet, as the weeks had slipped by, peace and quiet and freedom from the sort of harassment with Eric that had turned her days into waking nightmares were no longer enough. Something vital was missing from her life, a need that friends alone couldn't fill. What bothered her was the knowledge that it had taken Bennet Montgomery to teach her that.

She'd just finished pouring the coffee when a shocking postscript to her bout of self-analysis blazed across her mind: was it possible that her feelings for him ran deeper than mere attraction? That, for all she thought herself immune, that old cliché, love, was trying to sneak up and take her unaware?

Oh, Lord, she fervently hoped not! He would not be an easy man to love, even if she felt ready to take chances with her heart again. And yet that might explain why she sometimes dreamed about him, then lay awake the rest of the night with her imagination running wild, creating scenarios that owed very little to probability and an awful lot to wishful thinking.

Maggie scowled into her coffee cup, afraid that she'd diagnosed an incipient ailment without having the first idea how to cure it.

Bennet cleared his throat, and Maggie became aware that he was staring at her speculatively, rather like a dog debating the wisdom of tangling with a bad-tempered cat. "I suppose it wouldn't hurt me to put in an appearance at the barbecue," he muttered at last. "And I suppose you're right. It probably would be a good idea to bring Chris with me and expose him to a few of the locals, too."

The locals, indeed! Don't do them any favors, she was on the verge of snapping back because, apart from herself, the closest anyone else in town ever came to meeting Bennet or the rest of his household was every Saturday morning when his black sedan sped down the highway to Annisville—leaving behind nothing but a cloud of dust—and again late in the afternoon when it returned. But taking refuge in insults didn't help any longer. It was too late to try to dislike him. "You might even enjoy yourself," she offered instead.

He cast her a dubious glance. "I don't know, Maggie. Village picnics aren't exactly my style."

Remembering the reception where she'd first met him, she supposed he was right. There wouldn't be imported caviar, smoked sturgeon or an endless flow of Möet & Chandon at Saturday's gathering, but there would be warmth and laughter and sincerity. She knew which she preferred. "You'll never find out unless you try one."

They left it at that, with nothing being settled, because Christopher came back outside just then.

The early mist had barely risen from the lake on Saturday morning before preparations for the barbecue got under way. By noon, a makeshift grill and spit were in place over a pit of coals in the sand. Four long trestle tables had been set up under the trees, and Mrs.

Murphy's old copper boiler had been hauled out of retirement once again and filled with ice to keep the beer cool. By two o'clock, the beef was basting in its own juices over the fire, the rest of the food had started to appear, and people were beginning to party in earnest.

When neither Bennet nor Chris had shown up at five o'clock, Maggie stopped expecting them and tried shaking off her disappointment in a strenuous game of volleyball. Her team was ahead by a nose and within sight of victory when, diving for a low ball, she experienced the feeling that she was being bathed in something warmer and much more personal than the late afternoon sun. Looking up, she discovered Bennet, no more than ten feet away on the sidelines, standing a little apart from the other spectators.

It was a Bennet she hardly recognized. Gone were the tailored pants she'd grown used to seeing him wear, replaced by a pair of shorts that were a far cry from ragged denim cutoffs, perhaps, but were shorts just the same, revealing legs that deserved to be shown off. Instead of some urbane stranger passing briefly through town, he looked, for the first time, almost as if he belonged. And, for a change, he didn't turn away when he saw that she'd noticed him.

"Maggie—hey!"

She'd been staring. The disappointed chorus from her teammates and the cheering section recaptured her attention a fraction too late. The other side took the point and the game, and she was left to brush the sand from her knees and suffer the good-natured insults being rained on her head.

"That was all your fault," she accused Bennet, as everyone else drifted off to find refreshment.

"I can't imagine why. I only just got here and was simply standing around absorbing a little local culture and minding my own business." Squinting against the sunlight reflecting off the water, he grinned at her, the picture of casual, easy elegance. "Though you do seem to make a habit of flinging yourself at my feet."

"Oh, such vanity!" she snorted. "I didn't even know you were here."

"Then how come you were staring so hard you forgot to pay attention to the game?"

"Because you look so normal," she shot back.

He raised pained brows. "Should I be flattered?"

"You should offer to get me something cool to drink and stop letting me say things I'll regret in the morning. And yes, you should be flattered. You look—" gorgeous, fantastic, incredibly sexy "—nice."

His gaze roamed warmly over her again. "You look rather nice yourself, Maggie."

She looked a mess, her nose all shiny, her hair coming loose from its braid, and her damp swimsuit making her itch. But worse than that, the way he was looking at her was making her blush all the way up from her neck. "I should get changed. I hate the feel of wet clothes."

Reaching out, he stopped her escape by closing his fingers lightly over her shoulder. "I wish you wouldn't. I like the look of you just the way you are."

For once, the tension was missing and they were just an ordinary man and woman testing the perimeters of a relationship that had nothing to do with anything but the here and now. It might have been the setting or the generally relaxed atmosphere created by a congenial group of people that made the difference. Maggie didn't really care. She was too busy marveling to waste time analyzing. Until Edith Caverley approached, dedicated curiosity begging to be satisfied written all over her face.

"Bennet," Maggie said, confusion making her forget that she only allowed herself to call him by his first name in her most private fantasies, "let go of me or you'll have the whole town buzzing. My neighbor from across the street is bearing down on us and, if she sees you hanging on to me like this, the next thing you know we'll be practically engaged!"

Maybe it was the hushed way she spoke that made her words come out sounding as though she attached undue significance to his touch. Whatever the reason, another of those moments suddenly hung between them, suspended on implications of intimacy so fragile and fraught with tension that Maggie was almost afraid to breathe. But she had to, if only to explain what she'd really meant. "I don't mean that *I* think we . . . I mean, I know *you* don't—"

"Stop digging yourself in deeper and go and get changed, Maggie," he cut in gently. "I'm not socially retarded. I can cope with your neighbor without insulting her or letting her coerce me into anything I don't want to do." His fingers slackened, releasing her an inch at a time. "Just hurry back."

Casual enough words, but the unspoken message in his eyes would have stoked the fires of gossip for a month, had Edith been close enough to interpret it. Things, Maggie thought distractedly, were getting dangerously out of hand.

Her shoulder burned from his touch, the heat flaring down her arm. She swallowed, tongue-tied. Where were all those glib and snappy comebacks when she really needed them? "I thought you'd decided to bring Chris with you," she managed feebly.

"I had, but he isn't feeling very well. A bit of an upset stomach, a slight temperature. Nothing serious except too much sun, I suspect."

She tried to look reproving. "You don't sound particularly concerned."

"I'm not." He stepped closer. "Mrs. Marshall's staying home with him, so he's in good hands, and I'm not about to waste a heaven-sent opportunity like this focusing my attention where it's not really needed, when I have other, more pressing things on my mind."

"Heaven-sent opportunity...?" Maggie repeated faintly, because he had entwined his fingers with hers, and his eyes were hungering over her face in a way that made her very short of breath all at once.

"Have dinner with me, Maggie," he suggested in a low, intense voice. "Sit under a tree and share the sunset with me. Just for once let's act like normal people who haven't forgotten how to enjoy life or each other."

A week ago, she'd have given her right arm for all the mixed signals to come to an end and for him to be the straightforward man she'd first met. But that was before she'd come face-to-face with the complicating possibility of falling in love with him. So, instead of responding like the mature adult she liked to think she was, she reacted to his request like a teenager, all trembly inside, all flushed out. Shivering with strange fever. Dear Lord! "I'll have to get changed first," she croaked.

"Go." He smiled and gave her a little push, then turned to meet Edith's eager face, his manner at once that curious blend of spontaneous charm and controlled arrogance that was, Maggie belatedly realized, one of the fronts he assumed to hide his natural shyness. "How do you do? You probably already know who I am, but let me introduce myself, anyway. I'm Bennet Montgomery."

He'd identified himself to her in much the same way, that afternoon just over a month ago when he'd found her sprawled on his doorstep. A timely reminder in more ways than one, Maggie scolded herself, lifting the flap of the tent set up as a ladies' changeroom for the day.

She hadn't known him much more than six weeks, a span of time so brief that it undermined any credibility she might attach to her feelings for him. True, she liked him, but anything deeper was out of the question. Six weeks was about the right time for a schoolgirl crush to blossom, or even a post-adolescent infatuation to take shape, but anything more—in a woman of her age and experience? Absurd!

CHAPTER SIX

BENNET half expected her to disappear and not come back. She'd looked appalled at the turn their conversation had taken, which didn't really surprise him. He was a little appalled himself. But, coming upon her like that, lithe and tanned in her royal blue swimsuit that fitted so sleekly, with the sun pooling a halo of light around her blond head, had made him forget that he'd intended to use Chris as an excuse to put in only a brief appearance at the barbecue. Something had broken free inside him and let loose feelings that he'd been sure he had well in control.

"She's a lovely young woman, our Maggie," Edith Caverley observed, following the direction of his gaze and nodding at the tent flap behind which Maggie had disappeared.

"Indeed." But a complication he'd spent the last month telling himself he didn't need.

"So good with the little ones."

True. If he was smart, he'd remember that was the only reason he'd allowed her to intrude so far into his life. "Hmm," he replied noncommittally.

But Edith Caverley, he soon realized, was not a woman to be easily discouraged. "There's more to her than meets the eye, you know. Hidden depths, you might say."

There always were with women, that was the whole trouble. Something always surfaced with them when it was too late to get out of the line of fire. He ought to know. He had the scars to prove it.

"Are you married, Mr. Montgomery?"

"No," he said, and managed to curb himself just in time from adding, Thank God!

"Neither is Maggie."

"Really?" A sensible man would question why not. Heaven knew, she was the right age. Bright, interesting, beautiful. *Desirable.*

He glowered. Enough of that rubbish! "Perhaps she's a dedicated career person."

Edith chuckled. "And content to live in Sagepointe, dear boy? I hardly think so."

He had to agree. Maggie and Sagepointe just didn't fit as neatly as they should, somehow. He might have been fooled into believing otherwise if he hadn't seen the inside of her house. All that artwork, that priceless and beautiful furniture, bespoke more than a passing familiarity with money and culture. She'd admitted to having attended one of his concerts, to having met Francis at a post-performance reception, but he knew for a fact that such invitations weren't handed out indiscriminately. Patrons were courted as much for the generosity of their financial support as they were for their appreciation of fine music. Yet Maggie's lifestyle was simple, her clothes often charming but unremarkable. As for jewelry, he couldn't recall seeing her wear anything but a plain gold chain and watch.

"Perhaps," he said, airing his private hope—or was it really a fear? "she's not all she seems to be."

Edith's nose quivered with excitement. "What *do* you mean, Mr. Montgomery?"

He wished he knew. And if Maggie ever came out of that blasted tent and rescued him from this woman with the beady, inquisitive eyes of a magpie, he intended to find out, because there'd be no peace of mind for him until he did. He needed reasons not to be obsessed by her, not to be lying awake in the small hours of the morning, imagining . . .

At thirty-eight, he ought to know better than to airbrush reality with fantasies that probably couldn't survive the cold light of day. Women were impressed by money and fame. Drape them in diamonds and furs, show them a good time, make headlines with them on the front page of the society section, and they'd gaze up at him and hang on a man's every word as though it were the result of divine inspiration. Flatter him, admire him, pretend to love him, even. But let the going get tough and the women got going—to greener pastures.

Maggie wasn't like that.

"You were saying, Mr. Montgomery?"

Afraid his thoughts were showing too plainly on his face, he rearranged his expression. "Nothing." He smiled blandly. "It's a beautiful day, isn't it, Mrs. Caverley?"

"So far." She sagged at his determined change of subject, disappointment manifest in her expression. "But there's a storm brewing."

She was right. Across the lake, thunderheads towered on the horizon, purple and angry looking. There would be a spectacular sunset, if the rain held off. "I suppose the farmers won't mind," he remarked. "It's very arid country up here."

"Wait until you experience one of our winters. Very long and very cold." Mrs. Caverley brightened as a new avenue of discovery opened. "Where did you live before coming here, Mr. Montgomery?"

He slewed his glance once more towards the tent, and replied vaguely, "Here and there. I've traveled a great deal."

"With your little boy?"

He sighed with barely concealed exasperation. His inventiveness was wearing thin, and all the reasons for remaining aloof from local society bore down upon him with renewed validity. He could imagine with what relish Edith Caverley would seize upon the fact that Chris was not his son, what mileage she'd make of the discovery that the boy's father had signed him over to his uncle like a piece of unwanted baggage. Yet it was becoming increasingly obvious that, sooner or later, these details were bound to emerge.

Bennet kicked at the sand and scowled moodily. He'd been a fool to think he'd find anonymity in a small town, and an even bigger fool to be entertaining notions of romance with one of its residents, about whom he knew nothing except that she was good with children. He wished he were a thousand miles away, safely out of the reach of a blue-eyed, golden-haired temptress who made him want to believe in honesty and truth again.

What had Edith said to bring about his change of mood? Maggie wondered in resignation, recognizing the downspin of the emotional yo-yo once again. Bennet seemed preoccupied and annoyed, as though beset by a problem of monumental and far-reaching proportions.

Except to say, "Rare, please," when asked how he liked his beef, he didn't speak another word until they were through the food line. Carrying plates for both of them, he navigated a path through the crowd, leaving Maggie to follow with two plastic wineglasses and three-quarters of a bottle of burgundy that he'd lifted right from under Mrs. Murphy's teetotaling nose.

"Over there," he muttered, nodding to a spot far enough down the beach to discourage anyone else from joining them.

Maggie was surprised, half expecting him to have changed his mind about having dinner alone with her. Something had certainly changed during the time it had taken her to shed her wet swimsuit and spruce herself up with the aid of a hairbrush and a tiny mirror taped to one of the tent poles.

"Did Edith give you the third degree?" she asked, when they were settled with their backs against a log and their plates on their laps.

"She tried." He saluted her with his glass of wine, wintry humor glinting briefly in his eyes. "She didn't get very far."

"She's harmless, you know."

"So are mosquitoes." He slapped at one attempting to settle on his thigh. "But tiresome, all the same, and there's no escaping either of them." Stabbing his fork into his beef, he hacked off a chunk and contemplated it moodily. "It makes me wonder why anyone would choose to live here."

It seemed a strange observation, coming from a man who had presumably moved to Sagepointe voluntarily. Maggie stole a glance at him. "You chose to."

"That's because I'm hiding," he replied without hesitation, and turned his head to skewer her with his unblinking gaze as he flung his next question at her. "What's your reason?"

"I—er—" she swallowed, annoyed that he was treating her with such overt suspicion, and even more annoyed at herself for reacting so guiltily when she had no cause "—I like it. What do you mean, *hiding*?"

"I got tired of being in the public eye. I felt it was time to drop out of sight. *Why* do you like it here?"

Why was he simmering with irritation, as though he were itching to pick a fight and had chosen her as the unlucky adversary? "Because it's real."

"Real?" He practically sneered. "What does that mean?"

"People are exactly the way they seem, straightforward, simple, if you like. They care about each other, accept each other for what they are, and never mind that no one is perfect. Edith's nosy and there are times when she gets on everyone's nerves but, if she were to fall down her stairs and break her leg, there isn't a soul in town who wouldn't do what he could to help her out."

"Hypothetically touching, I've no doubt, but you're surely not trying to tell me you choose to live here in case you fall and break a leg?"

"Of course I'm not!" Maggie took a firmer grip on her patience. The man was worse than a fractious child! "I'm saying that no one really cares that Edith's such a gossip, because there's no real malice in her, and anyway, no one has any dark secrets they want to keep hidden."

"Anyone old enough to have a past has secrets of one sort or another, Miss Jones. I know I do, and I defy you to look me in the eye and tell me you don't."

"Well, I—"

"For example, why have you cast yourself in the role of spinster schoolmarm, looking out for other people's children, when most women your age are busy raising babies of their own?"

Oh, he could be cruel, sometimes! "Because—"

"And why are you pretending that you find the company of these people stimulating?" He waved his knife at the mob gathering around Howard Stills and Walt Murphy, who were easing into the singsong with "Clementine." "There isn't a man here under fifty able to discuss anything more cosmopolitan than the latest price of cattle feed."

"There isn't a man here that I need to—" She stopped and bit back the response he'd almost goaded her into making . . . *that I need to be afraid of.*

But he wasn't about to let her off so easily. "What? What were you going to say, Maggie?"

"Nothing important." She waded her way stolidly through a mouthful of beef and realized it might as well have been cardboard for all she was enjoying it.

"I hate answers like that," he said through clenched teeth.

Maggie flung down her fork. "You know what? I'm not having much fun any longer, and you don't seem to be, either. Why don't you sit in splendid, cosmopolitan isolation, and contemplate the esoteric splendor of the diurnal rotation of the earth?"

Collecting her glass and plate, she prepared to get to her feet. "Personally, I prefer to sit with ordinary people and enjoy the sunset."

Bennet's hand shot out and hauled her back down beside him, upsetting the bottle of burgundy at the same time. The wine soaked away until all that remained of it was a dull red stain on the surface of the pale sand. "Go waste your sarcastic wit on those clods you were playing ball with, you mean? Like hell!"

"Clods?" she gasped. Deceptively elegant, his fingers held the strength of tempered steel, and she refused to lower herself to the futile indignity of trying to break away. Instead, she focused her eyes unwaveringly on his hand. "Compared to you and your tactics, Mr. Montgomery, they behave like perfect gentlemen. Let me go, at once."

As if he suddenly realized he was acting like a fool, he released her. "Good God," he muttered, staring at her in astonished dismay, "I think I'm jealous!"

It was the last thing she expected to hear him say. She could have used his anger to boost her own indignation, deflected his scorn with contempt, and successfully fooled both of them into believing she didn't give a damn what he thought about anything. But his softly uttered remorse completely disarmed her. "I can't imagine why," she said. "They are just boys."

He nodded. "And you are a woman."

But a woman unlike any he'd known before, truly content with simple pleasures. At first, when he'd seen her with Chris, he'd thought she was putting on an act for the sake of the child. But in his heart he knew, after hours of observing her from a distance—hours that he should have spent practicing for his upcoming recording session—that this was only partly true. She had a capacity for enjoying life that was sincere and entirely unselfconscious.

Hardly reason, though, for him to be behaving like a teenager in the throes of unrequited puppy love. It had shocked him, that sudden rush of jealousy, but he was honest enough to acknowledge that it had been fermenting ever since he'd stood watching her tumble about in the sand with strangers—men, some of them—bodies brushing, arms and legs touching.

Oh, hell, he was *worse* than a teenager! He'd be writing bad poetry next.

In the background, the sound of a harmonica wailed against the tinny beat of a banjo, and a chorus of voices begged Tom Dooley to hang down his head and die. Not bad advice, Bennet thought wryly, and gestured again, attempting to understand the incomprehensible. "Does Miss Margaret Cecilia Jones really like all this? The unpretentious fun and friendliness?"

"Yes," she answered without reservation. "It's what I need. I'm happy here in a way I never thought I'd ever be again."

"Even though you're alone?"

"Unattached, you mean?"

"Yes."

She braced herself, knowing that he deserved at least partial return on his own candor, even if it meant reopening old wounds. "I was married once."

So these, then, were the memories that sometimes darkened her eyes to shades of midnight. Bennet pushed aside his plate, his appetite suddenly gone. Whatever else he had thought to discover, he had not expected this. "A husband?" He could barely articulate the word around the renewed jealousy clogging his throat.

"An ex. I've been divorced for nearly three years, almost as long as I was married."

Time enough for her to have forgotten him, whoever he was. Unless... This time, the words were even more difficult to speak. "Do you still love him?"

She hesitated. Love Eric? It seemed a ludicrous suggestion from this perspective in time, yet once, when she was very young and very gullible, she'd thought she did. How long had it taken for that naive and unlikely adoration to sink into fear? A year? Two? "No."

Bennet noticed the hesitation. "You don't seem sure."

"Oh, I'm sure," she whispered with strange bitterness. "I'm very sure indeed."

She looked haunted.

"It must have been a very painful time," he commented, "to cause you so much distress, all these years later."

"It was hell," she said, so quietly that he had to lean close to hear her. "I didn't know what evil really was until I married Eric."

Bennet reached for her hand and tucked it inside his. "Was it after that that you decided to come here?"

Maggie felt brittle under his touch, as though she were strung together with piano wire pulled so tight she might snap. "Yes." She let out a long, slow breath and bent her head. "I healed here. I suppose you could say I found myself again."

Her hair had swung forward, a sheet of sun-kissed silk hiding her profile. He wanted very much to sweep it back, to feel its cool softness against the palm of his hand, but there was a remoteness to her now that made him unsure.

He hadn't meant to upset her with his questions. He'd wanted only two things: to prove that there was nothing of substance beneath that alluring exterior, and to convince himself she was not what he wanted. But he had miscalculated on both counts. "Then don't

look back," he said. "Or, if you must, be grateful that
our separate pasts and heartaches have made us what
we are today and brought us together at this time, in
this place. That's what matters, Maggie."

She understood the words, but had to risk looking
at him to confirm the tenderness, the promise of passion, that she thought she heard in his voice. She had
to, even though in doing so she knew her own eyes
would reveal to him how desperately she wanted him
to care.

He saw. "Maggie…?" Her name whispered past his
lips, half invitation, half protest, as though a hundred well-entrenched doubts were fighting to retain a
stronghold they'd never expected to come under siege.

Across the lake, thunder growled a warning. Ignoring it, Maggie cast aside the inhibitions that were yet
another legacy of her marriage, and leaned toward
Bennet. She wanted to breathe in his scent, taste him,
touch him. She wanted to kiss him, desperately wanted
him to kiss her back. The depth of her wanting
stunned her, concentrating in a knot of tension so ur-
gent, it depleted her of the ordinary strength required
to hold open her eyelids. They fell shut, weighted by
a hunger she'd never known before.

Something wet and cool touched her face and was
followed in quick succession by other wet, cool drops,
not quite as gentle. As though, Maggie thought, her
eyes flying open with shock, the weather were determined to save her virtue, if not her sanity. Gathering
all its pent-up displeasure, the storm swept in, sand-
blasting them with wind, pelting them with rain, while

lightning streaked over the water in wicked, searching fingers, and the thunder roared its outrage.

The plastic wineglasses sailed across the beach, airborne. "Good Lord!" Bennet shouted against the din. "Where did this come from?"

Maggie's laugh was a hair's breadth short of hysterical. "Guardian angels, I think."

Dragging her to her feet with one hand, he scooped up her tote bag with the other. Already, down the beach, evidence of the barbecue was fast disappearing, as people loaded cars and trucks. Not everyone, it seemed, had been too distracted to notice the speed with which the storm had chosen to crash the party.

Bennet flung a glance their way. "They don't need us," he decided, and, with his hand still gripping hers, made a dash for the road. "Did you bring a car?"

"No."

"Neither did I. We'll just have to run for it."

Her house sat a couple of hundred yards to the other side of the school. By the time they reached her front porch they were soaked to the skin. Below them, the petunias lay in their flower bed with their faces pressed into the dirt. A premature twilight darkened the skies.

"I guess," Bennet said hoarsely, "this is where I say good-night and leave you to go inside and change yet again."

"Yes." Her reply was a thread of sound almost swallowed up by the drumming rain.

But he still had hold of her hand and, instead of letting it go, he reached out for the other one, too.

"Your hair is dripping wet. Make sure you towel it dry. I'd hate for you to catch cold."

It was hardly likely. That strange fever was back. She was surprised the raindrops didn't hiss as they snaked down the length of her throat to puddle between her breasts. He must be aware. Surely he could feel the heat, see the shallow breathing that was all her racing heart permitted?

"'Night," he said, and slid his hands up her arms until they found her shoulders. In the gloom, she could not see his face, only the shadow of him looming over her.

Either go now and let me live my life in peace, a voice inside her screamed silently, or stay and change it forever.

He heard. Without another word, he closed the mighty distance that separated them from everything that was orderly and predictable, and drew her hard against him.

Her head fell back, exposing the sweet, submissive curve of her throat. Her hair, plastered to her skull and dark as amber from the sluicing rain, revealed her features in all their stark and simple beauty. Lightning darted past the heavy foliage of a maple tree to spill briefly over her upturned face, making secrets of her eyes and mysteries of her mouth...mysteries he had to solve. It was more than he could do to walk away.

His lips were warm and hungry, and so sweetly persuasive that she found her own softening and opening beneath them. What might have lasted a second and then conceivably have been dismissed as nothing of moment strayed into a minefield of passion Maggie had never, in her wildest dreams, imagined. There on her front porch, his hands still on her shoulders and only his mouth delving into hers, he made love to her more thoroughly than she'd ever been loved before.

He knew he should stop, now, while he still could—that greed had a habit of backfiring and demanding interest beyond a man's capability to pay. But she was alive beneath his touch, her fire unspooling in ribbons until it flowed around her and around him in gentle, irrevocable bonds that no amount of restraint could ever unravel.

Just when he reached past her to open her front door, just how they found themselves inside with the rest of the world shut outside, was scarcely relevant. It was that other, invisible threshold they crossed that mattered.

Her bedroom gleamed softly in tones of white on white except for the corners that were misted purple with shadows. The bed, high and wide with brass rails, waited, piled with pillows covered in cool cotton slips. But she was all satin warmth awash with passion and created especially for him.

Bennet could not resist her. His tongue craved the drop of water that pooled in the hollow of her shoulder. His hands coveted the narrow tanned isthmus of her waist, knowing that, once he had conquered it, her breasts and hips were his for the taking. He hungered to test the fragile swath of skin that cloaked her inner thigh, and steeled himself to patience, for such a feast deserved to be savored.

But he had reckoned without the desire he had so carelessly ignited in her. It drove her without mercy, turning her hands into instruments of torture more exquisite than anything a mere man could hope to combat.

He didn't pretend to understand the emotions prowling the far corners of his mind. The feelings she aroused in him, the thoughts he'd entertained about her, made no sense. She was a stranger, an enigma. Yet at that moment he believed he would die if he were to lose her. Desire blended with a more enduring passion and smashed aside the reserves behind which he habitually hid.

His hands slid over her damp and willing flesh. She smelled of flowers and sunshine, of rain and wind and the pure, sweet air of the high country. He ventured a look at her face, saw rather than heard her mouth softly whispering his name. Momentum gathered inside him, a wild and violent force on the brink of detonation.

She moved, then. Reached up both arms, wound them around his neck, and drew him down to discover all of her—a sleek and pliant invitation he couldn't withstand. Her hair, drier now, swirled around them to hide the passions that glazed their eyes and made fools of their lungs.

She was a divorced woman who had done her best to honor her wedding vows. She knew that sometimes duty was not pretty or neat. She had become adept at turning off her mind, at enduring stoically those things a husband had a right to demand, without once allowing herself to question *her* rights.

She had adopted these fundamentals of survival so thoroughly that she had thought nothing could ever displace them. And yet, with the thunder still muttering its disapproval outside the window, she abandoned every last one because, this time, there was no question of obligation or subterfuge. This time there was Bennet. He stripped away the layers until she could not hide from herself or him, arousing in her a desire too willful to heed anything but its own driving need for gratification.

Suddenly, all the familiar landmarks receded and she found herself hurtling toward a new horizon. Terrified, she tried to negotiate the sweet undertow, willing to settle for mediocrity, the way she always had. But her body betrayed her, flinging itself joyfully toward destruction with her locked in a vacuum of loneliness so intense she could have wept. For an agonized twenty seconds or more she fought to stem the tide, heard a stranger's cry escape her, and knew she'd failed.

And then, suddenly, she was not alone at all. Bennet was there with her, heartbeat for heartbeat. His arms were strong and loving, his possession of her so complete that she knew his mark would stay with her the rest of her life, and he was murmuring in her ear, speaking a language she understood even though she'd never heard it before.

It brought the tears to life, had them streaming down her face. He knew about them before she did, was kissing them into oblivion before the sobs could be born. His ardor released her, but it was his tenderness that destroyed her, and she was glad to let it because, as the minutes rolled quietly by and the planet righted itself again in the vast order of the universe, a different Maggie emerged.

Bennet held her as if he was afraid she might break. She felt complete, fragile, cherished. As newly awakened as a virgin who'd just been handed the priceless gift of self-discovery by a man to whom she'd surrendered nothing.

She wanted to give to him, too, and turned to look at him where he lay sprawled beside her, one arm cushioning his head, the other flung possessively over her.

Perhaps her eyes revealed too much.

"Don't," he said, touching a finger to her lips. "It's too soon, too much, and—" he sighed and rolled away from her "—most likely too good to be true. Let's not spoil it with promises or declarations neither of us might be able to honor tomorrow."

CHAPTER SEVEN

WHEN Wendy Carlson-Lewis phoned early the next morning with an invitation to lunch in Vancouver, the sound of her soft, cultured voice brought back memories to Maggie that were at once pleasurable and painful.

She'd probably still be married to Eric if Wendy hadn't happened to drive up to the family compound the day that Maggie had found herself trapped outside the garage doors, with the Rottweilers, egged on by Eric, lunging at her from the end of their chains. His sadistic enjoyment of his wife's terror had caused something to snap inside his mother. "You have to get away from this," Wendy had insisted to Maggie later, her voice trembling with distress. "Please, darling girl, don't end up like me, too weak and afraid to make the break."

Maggie had been stunned by the admission. Wendy had always seemed so accepting of her subservient role as Mrs. Eric Carlson-Lewis Senior.

"We're possessions, you and I," Wendy had continued, "and, just like everything else they own, our husbands expect proper return on their investment."

"If you believe that, Wendy, then why haven't you left?" Maggie had asked.

"Because I fulfilled my function. I gave my husband four sons to carry on the line, which is all I was ever expected to do, and by then it was too late. It'll be the same for you, Maggie."

Except that it wouldn't be the same, as Maggie had been only too well aware, because she hadn't managed to produce an heir. Despite the most calculated efforts, she had failed to become pregnant and, as each successive month had rolled by without an announcement, Eric had become increasingly abusive. His "little pig-in-a-poke wife," he'd once called her, "good for nothing and sterile, to boot."

Wendy's love and support had become her lifeline. The friendship that had started on that dreadful day with the dogs had outlasted the divorce and all the messy publicity it attracted, but it was a friendship they celebrated in private. Neither Eric nor his father would have tolerated it, had they known about it.

That meant, of course, that the two women were able to meet only rarely, and Maggie thanked providential fate for bringing her former mother-in-law to town at this particular time. She'd lain awake half the night, thinking about Bennet and swinging between wonder and despair at what had taken place between them. What had prompted her to cast aside caution like that? Certainly not common sense, and surely not just rampant lust? Conflicting emotions swirled within her, robbing her of her usual ability to think rationally. Something shining and beautiful had happened, but, for reasons she couldn't fathom, Bennet had chosen to tarnish it with doubt. Was last night a beginning, or an end? The start of a love affair, or a one-night stand? She had no answers, and knew only that she needed a sympathetic, understanding ear, and that she could trust Wendy with her most closely held hopes and fears.

Within an hour of Wendy's call she was on the road, expecting that she'd be back in Sagepointe late that same evening. But fate wasn't so kind, after all. Unexpectedly, Eric showed up at his mother's hotel suite while her clandestine lunch with Maggie was in progress, and the scene he created, fraught with accusations and threats grown no less bitter with the passing of time, precipitated a heart attack in Wendy.

It was after dawn on Monday before her condition had stabilized enough for Maggie to feel able to leave her. It had been a wearing, anxious eighteen hours. The drive back to Sagepointe, over a winding, narrow pass, demanded her full attention. The sun was high, beating down from a cloudless sky; the heat was stifling, the glare blinding.

The town drowsed in the sweltering heat of early afternoon, but the old firs clustered around the big house lent it a shade that extended past the front door. The marble tiles of the entrance hall glimmered in cool welcome. From behind the closed door of his study, Maggie could hear the muted sound of Bennet's voice, apparently on the phone. The aroma of cinnamon and apples drifted from the kitchen to mingle with the heady summer scent of sweet peas in a vase on a nearby table. Upstairs someone moved to and fro in one of the bedrooms. There was no sign of Chris or Beau.

Slipping off her sandals, Maggie leaned for a moment against the front door, closed her eyes, and soaked up the tranquillity. Eric's ugliness couldn't touch her here. She was back in that safe other world again, Bennet's world, where she really belonged.

She might almost have fallen asleep on her feet had not Mrs. Marshall's hushed voice, heavy with relief, floated down from the head of the stairs to revive her. "You've shown up, Maggie. Thank the Lord!"

Pushing herself away from the support of the door, Maggie straightened up and fished about with one foot for her sandals. "You sound all in a dither, Mrs. Marshall. What's the matter?"

The housekeeper was too uncomplicated a woman to prevaricate. "He's fit to be tied," she said, jerking her head toward the study, "and all because something unexpected came up and you weren't here this morning to take charge of the boy, the way you were supposed to be."

"Oh, dear! Nothing's happened to Chris, has it?"

"Not exactly. He's with the dog and watching television in my room, even if it's not supposed to be good for him. At least it's keeping him entertained while I get things organized."

"Organized for what?" Maggie asked, but the sound of the telephone being slammed down in the study had the housekeeper scurrying back upstairs.

"Here he comes," she whispered, over her shoulder. "If I were you, I'd run for cover!"

It might have been better if she had but, before Maggie had both feet properly shod, the study door flew open and there stood Bennet. "Where the hell have you been?" he demanded, glowering down at her. Dressed in black to suit his mood, he loomed over her like a stern and unforgiving confessor addressing his penitent.

"In Vancouver," she replied, matching his brevity.

"I don't pay you to show up half a day late. You were supposed to be here at nine o'clock this morning."

"I was unavoidably detained."

"With two broken arms, no doubt, and therefore unable to pick up a telephone," he shot back. "Rather irresponsible behavior, if you ask me."

Pick up a telephone? Maggie thought of how quickly her pleasant visit with Wendy had turned into a nightmare, of how the rap on the hotel door that they'd both assumed heralded the arrival of room service with their lunch revealed Eric, instead. She remembered the rage in his eyes when he'd seen that it was his ex-wife his mother was entertaining, remembered, too, the hurled accusations, the insults. She thought she would never forget the sight of Wendy crumpling to the carpet, her skin the color of putty, her lips blue. What had followed had been indescribable, a slow-motion horror movie with the spectre of death in the leading role.

"I'm not asking you," she told Bennet stonily. "I'm conveying information and trying to give you an explanation."

"Why didn't you think about that yesterday?"

"Because it was Sunday," she said, when what she meant to say was, Because Sunday is my day off and you usually don't care what I do on my days off.

Her reply precipitated a fresh outburst of anger. "I know what day it was!" he roared.

Physically exhausted and emotionally drained, Maggie was in no mood to tolerate a temper tantrum from anyone, least of all the man who, if he had a single sensitive bone in his body, would welcome her rather more graciously, considering that the last time he'd seen her she'd been naked in bed with him. "You're shouting at me, Mr. Montgomery," she snapped, "which is a big mistake because, even if you were a lion tamer, I'm not the type to jump on command."

"Don't call me Mr. Montgomery! I'd have thought, all things considered, that we'd progressed beyond that point."

"I'd have thought so, too. But then, I'd also have thought you'd at least give me a chance to explain that a very dear friend of mine had a heart attack, and that I spent all yesterday afternoon and most of last night walking the floor of a Vancouver hospital, worried sick." Not to mention feeling horribly guilty that her confrontation with Eric was what had precipitated Wendy's illness!

"That's got nothing—" Bennet stopped short, his face a sudden mask of dismay, and reached for her. "Oh, Maggie, I'm sorry! Is your friend going to recover?"

His kindness was much harder to take than his anger. "Yes," she whispered, her eyes swimming in tears that had waited a small eternity to escape. "She's much better. The doctors are optimistic that she'll make a good recovery."

Bennet combed his fingers through her hair, smoothing it back from her forehead and tilting up her face so that his eyes could search hers. "I was worried, you know."

"There was no need."

"You just disappeared, and I thought perhaps I'd driven you away. I'm sorry I behaved the way I did."

She wished she were brave enough to ask, The way you behaved when? Today—or on Saturday night? Instead, she blinked away the tears and said, "Mrs. Marshall mentioned some sort of crisis. What's happened?"

"Nothing you need to worry about. You've got enough on your mind."

"No," she insisted. "I'm going to worry either way, so you might as well tell me and have done with it."

"I'm off to New York in a couple of hours to meet with my agent and finalize my European concert schedule. Normally, we're better organized, but we've just heard that Ivan Sergowski is expected in town." Noticing her blank look, he grinned faintly and shook his head. "The foremost pianist in the Soviet Union today, Maggie."

"He must have slipped through one of those appalling gaps in my musical education," she told him wryly. "How talented is he?"

"Enough to make working with him in concert one of the highlights of my career. Until recently he was never granted an exit visa from the USSR because of his outspoken anti-government views, but now that things are politically more relaxed he's free to travel. Unfortunately, every agent this side of the Iron Curtain is trying to secure dates with him, and I can't afford to miss this chance to meet him and make my pitch."

"So go with an easy mind," she said. "I'm here, and I'll be glad to look after Chris."

"Well, the thing is, when you didn't show up this morning and Chris found out I was going away, too, he threw a real fit. As far as he's concerned, when people leave him, they usually don't come back—you know, first his mother, then his father. I guess, because he's made so much progress in the last few weeks, we tend to forget how much he still has to overcome. Anyhow—" Bennet drew in a long, unhappy breath "—I decided to take him with me. It's not the most convenient solution for me, but it seemed the least traumatic for him. Now he's all fired up about flying on a real aircraft, and Mrs. Marshall's run off her feet getting his clothes sorted and packed."

Maggie felt bereft. She was losing both of them just when she needed them most.

Bennet noticed, but misunderstood. "Don't look so unhappy, Maggie. You'll be free to go back to Vancouver and be with your friend. Don't worry about the money, I'll—"

Go back to wherever it is you came from, Margaret, Eric had said. You've done enough damage and you're not welcome here.

"I wish you'd stop trying to buy me off!" she snapped at Bennet, startling him with her intensity. "The money's not important. And my friend doesn't need me now. She has her family by her side."

"I see." He regarded her thoughtfully for a moment. "Do you have any other plans?"

"Not at the moment, but please don't worry about me. I'll find something to do."

"I'm sure you will, Maggie. It's just that I was wondering if—er—" He paused, seeming almost diffident. "Oh, never mind. It's probably asking too much, anyway. It's not your sort of scene at all."

Fatigue had left her as short on patience as she seemed to be on intuition. "Whatever it is you're trying to say, Bennet, I wish you'd just spit it out and stop hemming and hawing like this."

Again, he looked taken aback at her tone, then he shrugged. "What the hell?" he muttered. "It can't hurt to ask. Would you consider coming with us? Before you refuse, let me tell you that I'm not asking as a favor to you, but to me. Chris knows you, he's comfortable with you, and I'll be able to leave him with an easy mind knowing he's in your care rather than left with a babysitter." He grimaced. "I can only imagine the scene I'd have to deal with when it came time to leave him with a stranger."

Maggie had to agree. She remembered well enough her own first meeting with Chris, and not for its happy outcome.

"There are a hundred things you can do to keep him entertained in New York," Bennet went on persuasively.

"New York in August is like a steam bath," she said, trying to cover up her absolute delight that he'd asked her to go along on the trip. It's for his convenience, not the pleasure of your company, she reminded herself.

"You could go on a harbor cruise, or for a ride down the river. Take Chris to F. A. O. Schwarz—he'll be fascinated by all the toys, and the store's air-conditioned! And we'll be in the city only about three days before we move on to Long Island. Sergowski is a houseguest of associates of mine who live out at the Hamptons. They have a beautiful summer home on the beach." He let loose that winning smile that turned all her powers of resistance to liquid acquiescence. "It'll be much pleasanter there, Maggie. Sea breezes, lobster feasts, walks along the shore. Think about it!"

"But I don't have a flight reservation," she said, wanting nothing more than to give in to his flagrant bribery, but feeling she should offer at least token resistance.

"That's no problem," he assured her. "If you can be ready to leave here in—" he flicked a glance at his watch "—oh, let's say an hour and a half, to be on the safe side, I'll take care of the travel arrangements."

"I can be ready," she said, resistance at an end.

He smiled again, pleased with his victory. "Then get going!"

She was halfway to the door when he called her back. "Oh, by the way, if you've got something a bit more formal for evenings, you might want to toss it in your suitcase." He eyed her denim skirt and short-sleeved cotton blouse, her bare, suntanned legs and casual, flat-heeled sandals. "Not that I don't think you always look charming, but the Prescotts dress for dinner, even when they're slumming it out in the country. However, if you don't have anything suitable, don't worry about it. You can go on a shopping spree in Manhattan."

It was Maggie's turn to smile. She could have stocked a small boutique with glamorous leftovers from her married days. Most of her ordinary, everyday clothes had been outworn, but she'd had little use for the designer cocktail dresses, evening gowns, satin shoes and beaded bags that filled one end of her closet. She'd have no trouble at all finding "something a bit more formal" to wear at the Prescotts'. She could even toss in a bit of jewelry to dazzle them, and, if it had been December instead of August, she had a couple of furs that could probably have used an airing. Bennet had no need to worry that she'd embarrass him by looking like a poor country cousin.

"I'll find something," she promised him.

New York was every bit as hot and humid as she'd expected. Maggie saw very little of Bennet, and when he was around he was preoccupied. Keeping Christopher

entertained and out of his uncle's hair taxed her imagination to the limit. In the end she abandoned most
of her plans to take Chris out in the city. The crowds
and noise terrified him, and the heat left him tired and
bad-tempered. It seemed best simply to do the same
things they did at home, and throw in a few little treats
to make it seem like a holiday. Bennet had booked
them into the Plaza, and their suite opened onto its
own private terrace. It was as cool up there, in the
shade of a patio umbrella, as it was anywhere else in
Manhattan.

On the fourth day they left for Long Island, arriv-
ing late in the afternoon. Maggie had spent a little time
in the Hamptons when she was married to Eric, and
knew that it was a summer playground for the wealthy,
but even she was unprepared for the opulence of the
Prescott home. Situated on three acres of land, atop
a gentle rise and looking out over the Sound, it was the
sort of rambling, gracious house designed for entertaining. There were wraparound verandas set with
white wicker furniture, a tennis court and swimming
pool, a croquet lawn, a gazebo, and a dock to which
was moored a sleek powerboat equipped for water
skiing.

Inside the house, the floors were polished maple
strewn with Chinese rugs, the furnishings a daring
mixture of New England antique, chinoiserie and art
deco. From the gardens, the perfume of old-fashioned
roses and lavender joined forces with scented stock
and drifted through the open windows of the high-
ceilinged rooms. Maggie knew that, at night, the

sound of the waves rolling up the beach would be more soothing than a lullaby. It was a magical spot, a place in which to dream and reminisce, a place to fall in love.

The Prescotts were strangers, yet she found them all too familiar. James, she estimated, was probably close to fifty, but he took great pains to appear forty. Deeply tanned and fit, with becoming touches of gray at his temples and a smile worth a small fortune, he was handsome enough to pass for a movie star. His handshake was firm, his manner expansive, his waistline very trim.

His wife reminded Maggie of a hummingbird, tiny, exotic and inexhaustible. She was relentlessly vivacious. "Call me Pippa, darling," she squealed, reaching up to kiss Maggie on both cheeks the moment she emerged from the car. "Bennet, darling, she's quaint! Wherever did you find her? Look at that hair—I would kill for that hair! And the boy, Bennet—" She waggled fingers tipped with scarlet and heavy with diamonds, and shook her head. "Precious!" she declared. "There simply isn't any other word to describe him. Will he let me kiss him?"

"No," Christopher said with unmistakable clarity, and clung to Maggie's skirt.

"He must be tired," Pippa decided, turning to Maggie with undimmed good humor. "Put him to bed, darling—Binky will show you where—then wash your sweet face and come down to the terrace. We're having drinks with Sergie."

Maggie felt it was time to assert herself. "Don't wait for me, please, Pippa. I'll stay and get Chris settled. I might even take a nap myself."

"Well, darling, of course, whatever makes you happy. Take a bath, give yourself a manicure, a facial, the works—I'll send Binky in with one of my Thai mudpacks. Just don't forget, cocktails at eight, dinner at nine—unless, of course, you'd rather eat in your room, with the boy?"

"I think Maggie will be up to socializing with adults, by then," Bennet observed with thinly veiled irony, "but it's probably a good idea for Chris to be served supper in his room. He's not used to all this excitement, and an early night won't hurt. Don't you agree, Maggie?"

"Yes," she replied shortly, and, taking Christopher's hand, followed their hostess up the steps and into the airy interior of the house where Binky waited. Pippa probably meant well, but Maggie could do without the patronizing.

The bedrooms were enormous and luxurious. Gauzy drapes fluttered in the breeze coming through the window. Maggie's room was decorated in shades of pink and ivory. Deep rose silk covered the walls, the carpet was a tender blush of color, the lampshades and bedspreads matched exactly the bouquet of miniature gladioli on the ivory lacquered dressing table.

Chris's room, separated from hers by a bathroom, was all soothing greens, from palest jade to rich emerald, but what delighted him most was the small four-poster bed and the set of tiny antique cars parading across the bookcase. Whatever else her shortcomings, Maggie thought, Pippa had flawless taste in interior design.

That evening, Maggie chose the white chiffon dress with the shirred hemline that showed just enough leg to be alluring and the neckline that was so high and virginal, it was pure temptation all by itself. She left her hair straight and loose so that it hung over one shoulder, and restricted her jewelry to pearls. She touched Diva perfume to her wrists and ankles and the nape of her neck, swept lilac shadow fleetingly over her eyelids, and darkened her lashes with mascara. She finished by outlining her mouth with a coral gloss that left her lips looking as if they'd just been kissed. And when she was ready to go downstairs and take Bennet by storm, Chris woke up from a nightmare and wouldn't let her leave.

"Bogeymans," he wailed, staring fearfully around his canopied four-poster.

By the time she had reassured him and rocked him back to sleep, it was almost ten o'clock and she felt as rumpled as she was sure she must look. It made a lot more sense to change into a robe, send her apologies to her hostess, and ask for a tray to be sent up to her room. Perhaps it was just as well, she told herself. She was too old to think she could catch a man's eye by showing a bit of leg, and ought to be too wise to think she wanted to. Bennet had made no further reference to their lovemaking and, if she was any judge of character, he wished to forget it had ever taken place.

Within the hour she was in bed herself. The connecting doors through the bathroom stood open so that Chris wouldn't feel so isolated in his room, and she'd left a small night-light by his bed. The sound of the sea was every bit as soothing as she'd known it would be.

There was no telling what time it was or how long she'd been asleep when she was awakened by a slight sound from his room. Not bothering with her robe, she slipped quietly out of her bed and went to check it out. She found Bennet, his shadow grotesquely elongated, standing by the four-poster and looking down at the sleeping child. He held his dinner jacket in place over his shoulder by one thumb. He had loosened his bow tie and unfastened the top studs of his dress shirt. Even though his face was turned away from her, Maggie could tell from his posture that he was discouraged. It was all she could manage not to go to him, to run her hand gently over his face and hair, and offer to share whatever burdens he carried in his soul.

He seemed to sense her presence. "Why aren't you asleep?" he whispered, without lifting his head.

"What time is it?"

"Almost one in the morning." He closed his eyes and rotated his head in a slow circle. His lashes cast a ridiculously long shadow on his cheek. "It has been a long and tedious evening. You didn't miss much."

I missed you, she thought, and felt her heart stall when he turned and looked at her, his gaze serious and intent, as though she'd said the words aloud. The air between them almost vibrated.

"Can we talk?" he asked, motioning with his head in the direction of her room.

Say no, her common sense begged silently. She paid no heed. "Yes," she said.

CHAPTER EIGHT

A FULL moon turned the night luminous and flung sharp-edged patches of silver across the floor. Nothing else in the room had color, but Bennet could see her as clearly as if it were day. Maggie wore a nightgown made of something filmy and soft that floated around her in such a way as to make her appear almost ethereal.

The tension hummed. "What did you want to talk to me about?" she asked, and her voice, pitched low, stroked along his nerve endings, inciting responses he'd sworn he'd never again allow her to provoke.

"I just wanted to apologize."

He sensed her look of inquiry from the tilt of her head. "Apologize? For what?"

"For abandoning you with Chris all evening. I'm sorry you were left to deal with him alone. I hadn't intended, when I asked you to travel with us, that you should be his round-the-clock nanny."

She shrugged, and the hemline of her gown lifted and foamed in gentle waves around her ankles. "I like looking after him, and if I didn't do it who else would? Pippa?"

"You don't like her," he surmised, and found himself almost holding his breath for her reply. She didn't know how much weighed on her answer.

"I have no reason to dislike her," she replied judiciously. "I just don't have much in common with women like her, that's all."

"What kind of woman is she, Maggie?" he asked, fascinated by the easy grace with which she sank onto the broad window seat and rested her head on one hand.

"The kind who likes to talk about the places she's seen, the people she knows, the things she owns—things money can buy, as if they're the only things in life that really matter."

"Some people would say they are."

She tilted her head again, and her hair fanned out to caress her shoulder. "Are you testing me, Bennet?"

He supposed he was. In any case, it seemed best to keep talking. Silence led into deep and dangerous waters. "Did you know," he said, strolling across to where she sat and propping himself against the window frame, "that I was once engaged to Pippa's cousin?"

"No," she replied, growing so still that the moon caught her profile and flung it on the wall in perfect cameo.

"It was about six years ago. We were to be married in the spring, a huge, elaborate affair in New York. But the winter before, I'd injured my spine in a helicopter accident, and spent the next four months in a body cast. For a while the doctors thought I wouldn't walk again."

He heard her indrawn breath, saw the shadow of her breasts rise in shock.

"Bennet, how awful!"

"It never occurred to me that they were right, but my dear bride-to-be decided to hedge her bets, just in case. While I began the long and arduous road back to recovery, she was seen about town on the arm of one man after another, all of them rich and extremely eligible. She couldn't spend time with me, she explained in a letter. She was too tenderhearted, and being around sick people upset her too much."

He laughed quietly. "Of course, when I walked out of that hospital under my own steam and picked up my life right where I'd been forced to leave off, she realized that marrying me wasn't going to mean living in obscurity and playing nursemaid to a cripple, and underwent a swift change of heart. She reevaluated the whole situation and decided to go with her first choice."

"How did you feel?"

He paused before answering, remembering with bitter humor his homecoming. "When you have nothing much to do for four months but stare at the ceiling and think, you view life a lot differently. I'd had time to come to my senses. When she showed up at my door, full of remorse, I released her from her commitment. Seeing her meal ticket about to disappear a second time, she reacted as I should have expected, and threatened to sue me for breach of promise."

"Oh, Bennet! What did you do?"

"Paid her off, of course. Made her an offer she couldn't refuse."

"But you must have been terribly hurt," Maggie murmured. "How could you still remain friends with Pippa?"

"Because you're quite right in your assessment of her. She's an acquirer, especially of people. She cultivates them without regard for their integrity or hers, as long as their names are newsworthy and will create a stir when she drops them among her international associates. The day I decide I'm through with public life I'll be persona non grata in this house. In the meantime, I'll use her as ruthlessly as she uses me."

"All this," Maggie said, and he wondered if he imagined the forlornness in her voice, "to punish her cousin? You must still be in love with her."

"After six years?" He gave a snort of laughter and resisted the urge to run his fingers through her hair. Better not to let the conversation get physical. "That wouldn't be love, Maggie, it would be obsession. No, I cured myself of her a long time ago, and learned a valuable lesson, too."

"Then why are you still so bitter?"

"Bitter?" His gaze swung to the star-washed ocean and settled on the broad aisle of moonlight angling down from the northern sky. "Realistic is a better word, I think. She stripped me of all my romantic illusions."

"How cruel!"

"On the contrary, she did me a favor. I am two different people—one, the glamorous figure the public sees, and the other, a private and unremarkable man. She couldn't see that, of the two personas, the second is the more real. She didn't want to settle for ordinary merchandise when she thought she'd been sold something special, and I had no business expecting her to."

"Listen to you!" Maggie cried, springing up from the window seat. "Why do you always reduce everything, including yourself, to the level of a commodity that can be bought and sold? I hate it when you talk like that!"

Once upon a time he'd have found her innocence touching; now it merely aroused his suspicion. "Why?" he asked, with unfeigned mockery. "Because I won't sugarcoat reality with a lot of romantic ballyhoo? Face it, my dear Miss Jones, these days even those favoring marriage hedge their bets with pre-nuptial contracts. If that's not sticking a price tag on love and reducing it to merchandise, I don't know what is. My unlamented fiancée set her priorities in proper order well before a wedding could take place, which saved us both a lot of grief, down the road."

Maggie gave a soft moan of distress. "All women are not like her, Bennet," she whispered, reaching up to frame his jaw with cool, alluring fingertips.

Her touch set off an electrical charge that blew his resolve to smithereens. Before he had time to stifle the impulse, he'd trapped her hand and pulled her into his arms. "Aren't they?" he rumbled, his lips exploring her temples and straying down her cheek to her throat.

Her reply almost got lost between one ragged breath and the next. "No...!"

Caution slipped off the edge of the earth. Her long, slender neck bewitched him. He wanted to invade the shadowed cleft between her breasts. He wanted to slide his mouth over her shoulder and investigate every last vertebra that shaped the graceful column of her spine. He wanted her. *Oh, Lord, he wanted her!*

But could he trust her? He lifted his head. "Make me believe you," he demanded hoarsely, and slanted his lips across hers.

He was the one calling the shots, he kept reminding himself. Even when the straps of her nightgown seemed to slip aside of their own accord and suddenly there was nothing beneath his hands but her sun-kissed skin, he continued to delude himself. Let the gown flutter to the carpet like an exhausted butterfly, and all the sweet, flowery smells of shampoo and soap and body lotion conspire to tempt him! Let the savage hunger claw at him! He could resist them all. He knew the lure of the flesh was no match against the power of the intellect.

He thought he could gamble with control, let it run wild for a little while, then rein it in safely just this side of the point of no return. He thought he could put her to the test and escape unscathed himself.

And he almost succeeded. If only she hadn't opened her eyes and let him see the desire that left her irises as dark as rain-drenched pansies. If only she hadn't melted against him so urgently that motive and consequence blurred, and cause brought into effect a holocaust of emotion that undermined the validity of his every other concern. But she did both those things, and he forgot how much he feared her vulnerability, her lethal trust. He lost touch with everything but the siren song of passion that torched his senses.

"Bennet," she whispered, his name a prayer on her lips, and, like a drowning man far out of his depth, he felt the waters close over his head.

He sank with her to the bed, heard the mattress sigh. Felt her mouth cling to his, her arms ensnare him. She was even more alluring than he remembered. The taste of her, the cream-smooth texture, the drugging temptation of secrets she chose to divulge to him alone, joined forces against him, fine-tuning the instruments of his destruction until, with the simple brush of her hand down his ribs, she wrought a sudden stillness that left him trembling between heaven and hell. For a second he hung motionless, then, in a delirium of impatience, he peeled off his clothes and claimed her.

Not until he touched her did Maggie realize how desperately she'd hungered for him. His kisses warmed the little starved hollow at her throat, his hands defined her breasts and drew her to fit snugly against him in such a way that all her soft curves surged with anticipation against his powerful angles.

Hidden places grew alive and eager, and other, less secret parts, too: the soft triangle of hip that drew sensory pleasure like a magnet and left her blind with need; the base of her spine, where passion seemed to incubate until it could no longer be contained and shot through her body, igniting her; her hair, which seemed to take on a life of its own, reaching out silken threads to bind her to him. And, underscoring them all, the drumroll of desire that pulsed so relentlessly, she thought she'd die.

Moonlight blanched the ceiling enough for her to see his lean, spare beauty. He towered above her, his eyes locked to her face as he lifted each of her hands and imprisoned them above her head so that he could kiss her inner wrists with tender savagery.

He might have been a man at war with a thousand enemies, on the verge of winning all his battles—until she slid one hand free and touched him again, more intimately this time, creating a tremor so potent and devastating that his most sought-after victory slipped away before he had time to prevent it. He sank into her with a desperation and passion he could no longer deny, and she imprisoned him without mercy.

It was not a gentle or forgiving union. They dueled until their bodies gleamed with sweat and their hearts nearly burst trying to outrace each other. She knew the agony tearing at her possessed him, too. She could feel it in the thick and rapid pulsing that drew them both closer to oblivion.

She knew precisely when he gave up the struggle for control because the same insatiable force claimed her, too, and nothing, not even the end of the world itself, could rescue either of them. Soaring free of all that

shackled them in saner times, they cleared the strato-
sphere and shot united through time and space, one
bright new star staking a brief claim on heaven.

Afterward, for a precious half hour, she drifted
peacefully, cradled in Bennet's arms. Lassitude stole
along her aching limbs and restored her heart and
lungs to order. Then Chris called out for her, and
Bennet stirred.

"My cue to leave," he said, and, by the time she had
Chris settled again, her bed was empty and only the
warm imprint of Bennet's body was left to remind her
that he'd ever been there beside her.

She'd let it happen again, she thought in delayed
anguish. Governed by impulse and the willful de-
mands of a body she'd always believed to be entirely
biddable to her wishes, she'd left herself dangling on
a rope of uncertainty, with no knowledge of how far
she had to fall before she hit solid ground again. She'd
been party to the most intimate experience two human beings could share, one that involved so much
more than the baring of flesh. She'd exposed her soul
to Bennet. And, as if that weren't enough, she was
afraid of her feelings for him, and didn't have the first
idea of how he really felt about her.

"Expect nothing and you won't be disappointed,"
she told herself as she prepared to face him a few hours
later.

But he was charming and attentive, showing none
of that reserve or regret that he'd expressed the first
time they'd made love. "I'm going to be tied up with
Sergowski for about an hour," he said, joining her at

the buffet set up in the breakfast room, "then I'll be free. What do you say to spending the rest of the day with me?"

Surprised at the pleasure and relief that flooded through her, Maggie refused to confront where her emotions were leading her. Whether it was irresponsible or foolish suddenly didn't matter. Just this once she wanted to enjoy the present without having to worry about the price it might exact on her future.

There were long, clean stretches of pale sand, and sunshine. There was lunch in the shady courtyard of a secluded little restaurant in town. There was Chris screaming with terrified glee as the breakers rolled ashore and chased him to safety up the beach. And most of all, there was Bennet, his smile flashing in his sun-dark face, and his defenses down. It was not a day to ask for guarantees or promises. It was a time to be grateful, not greedy.

Pippa, resplendent in fuschia crêpe, stood waiting for them on the terrace when they at last arrived back at the house, her little feet in their jeweled shoes tapping impatiently. "Darlings—" she pouted "—it's after six. We were about to send out the coast guard. We thought you'd been lost at sea."

They stood before her, wind-tossed and barefooted. Bennet had used his shirt as a carryall for sandals and wet swimsuits. Chris toted a pail brimming over with shells, and a trailing branch of seaweed. Maggie's hair was stiff with salt. The three of them looked, she realized ruefully, like castaways.

Pippa's bright, birdlike gaze darted from one to the other of them, missing nothing. "Maggie, take the precious child upstairs and do with him whatever it is one does with a child when an adult evening is planned. And if you decide to come down for dinner tonight—"

"Maggie will be joining us tonight, Pippa," Bennet interjected shortly.

Pippa smiled radiantly. "Well, wonderful! But do try to come up with something dressy, Maggie. I've asked a few people to join us for dinner, including our new neighbors. She was a Hoyt before she married, and does all her shopping in Rome. I mean, no offense intended, darling, but I wouldn't want you to feel out of place."

Maggie smiled. "No offense taken, and I promise not to feel out of place." *Darling!*

"Oh, goodie!" Pippa smiled without a trace of malice or embarrassment. "Getting them to come to dinner is the social coup of the season for me. I don't want anything to spoil it.

Chris was too tired to put up more than token resistance to going to bed. He barely managed to stay awake to the end of his bedtime story, which left Maggie with more than an hour in which to prepare for the evening ahead.

She used every last second. After Pippa's little spiel, she intended pulling out all the stops, and was glad she'd included in her baggage the slinky black gown she'd worn to the Cannes film festival one year, and the sapphires that Wendy had given her for her twenty-fifth birthday. This was one time, she thought, swirling her hair into a smooth golden coil on top of her head, that she intended leaving Pippa at a loss for words.

The silk jersey of the dress whispered over her body, clinging to her like a second skin from bosom to thigh, then flaring out to support layers of ruffles from her knees to her ankles. Against the simple black, her skin gleamed like expensive satin. As for the sapphires in their diamond and platinum settings... Maggie swung her head and watched the pendant earrings fling out sparks of fire. Superlatives hadn't been invented that could match them for sheer magnificence. She felt ready for anything, from the top of her head to the soles of her feet in their three-inch high-heeled sandals. There was nothing, she thought gleefully, adding a last spritz of perfume to her throat and wrists, quite like being taller than the opposition when it came to the final showdown.

The guests were assembled on the terrace. Already, it was dusk. A thousand or more tiny colored lights strung through the trees turned the garden into a fairyland. Beyond, the sea murmured, a restless, shimmering purple taffeta shot through with silver.

"Darling," Pippa trilled, her eyes growing round with astonishment the moment they fastened on Maggie, "you've wrought a miracle! Come and meet everyone." She flung out one arm and her collection of cloisonné bracelets slid up to her elbow. "People, this is the adorable nanny I was telling you about.

Bennet, tell her how lovely she looks, instead of standing there with your mouth hanging open.''

Heads turned, gazes came to rest speculatively on the sapphires. Smiles grew wider, hands extended, mouths voiced welcome. Maggie—or her trappings—had passed muster.

Pippa's delight left her feeling rather small and ungenerous. ''Darling, I'm speechless!'' the hostess confided. ''I feel like a fool! Why did you let me rattle on about dressing up?''

Bennet recovered his composure. Expression inscrutable, he handed Maggie Dubonnet over cracked ice with a twist of lemon. ''What is all this?'' he muttered, eyeing her outfit as if he thought she had a snake concealed somewhere within its folds.

''A charade,'' she started to explain, but the stir of late-arriving guests drew his attention away.

''People,'' Pippa sang out, ''I want you all to meet our new neighbors, Paula and Kyle Fielding.''

Maggie turned to face the newcomers, and felt suddenly sick. In the space of seconds, the evening changed from a charade to a terrible case of déjà vu as her glance locked with that of the Fieldings and mutual recognition sprang to life.

''Margaret Carlson-Lewis!'' Paula Fielding exclaimed. ''Is it really you?''

Conscious of being the center of curious and unwelcome attention, Maggie strove to remain unruffled. ''Hello, Paula. How nice to see you again.''

''You know each other?'' Pippa squawked, clearly affronted at being upstaged. ''My heavens, Maggie, what else do you have hidden up your nonexistent sleeve tonight?''

"We met years ago," Paula Fielding replied. "Kyle, you remember Margaret, don't you? The governor's ball in Philadelphia, and the summer season in Newport?" She extended a smile to Bennet. "You're Bennet Montgomery, the conductor, aren't you? Forgive us for being so rude, but seeing Margaret here has taken us completely by surprise."

Bennet shook hands with Kyle. "I'm more than a little surprised myself," he remarked with patent sarcasm, and turned cold eyes on Maggie. "The governor's ball in Philadelphia, *Margaret*, the summer season in Newport, and the annual barbecue in Sagepointe? What a diverse and interesting life you lead!"

Kyle kissed Maggie on the cheek. "You dropped out of the picture so completely after the divorce, my dear," he said, "that we assumed you'd—er—that you—"

"I returned to Canada," Maggie said, putting him out of his embarrassed misery. The Fieldings had been on the fringe of the Carlson-Lewis social set in the old days, and had almost certainly heard the gossip surrounding her acrimonious divorce. She could well imagine how Eric had embellished his version of events. "I've lived in British Columbia for nearly three years."

"Then you must have heard about Wendy Carlson-Lewis's heart attack," Paula said. "She was taken ill in Vancouver, during a stopover on her way to the

Orient. Apparently, some hanger-on the family no longer wishes to patronize made some sort of horrible scene and poor Wendy just keeled over. Eric happened to be there, too, thank heaven, or dear only knows what might have happened. Both he and his father were dreadfully upset by it all."

"I was the other person with her at the time she was taken ill," Maggie said evenly, not in the least surprised that Eric had reshaped facts to suit his personal vanity.

"My dear!" Paula looked aghast. "I had no idea that you even associated with the family any longer. Why, Eric made it plain, when news of the divorce was first made public, that you had been . . ." She paused delicately, a flush creeping up her cheeks.

"Paid off?" Maggie supplied with quiet dignity, aware of Bennet standing at her side like a block of stone, and equally aware of how incriminating the conversation must seem to him. Surely he realized there was another side to it all?

"No, of course not!" Kyle insisted. "Paula, I wish, just once, that you'd try to keep your feet out of your mouth! Margaret, I apologize for my wife's lack of tact. Have you heard how Wendy's doing?"

"As a matter of fact, I phoned the hospital this morning, and she expects to be discharged some time next week. I understand she plans to convalesce at her sister's home in Arizona."

"Kyle, I believe Pippa wants us to meet her other guests," Paula observed with palpable relief.

As though he feared she might try to escape, too, Bennet clamped an iron hand over Maggie's wrist and steered her toward the garden. "And I believe I'd like to talk to you some place private," he growled in a low, savage voice. "I believe there are a few autobiographical facts you neglected to mention before, and I believe hearing your explanation for that omission will make for very interesting listening."

"There's no need to drag me off my feet," Maggie objected, almost tripping over her high heels. "I'm perfectly willing to tell you whatever you want to know without your having to resort to manhandling me. Bennet, stop it! People are staring!"

"I'll let you go the minute we're out of sight and hearing of that crowd up on the terrace," Bennet snarled, refusing to slow his pace or release her. "Trust me on that! But I don't intend having an audience because, regardless of what *you* might have to say, what *I* plan to get off *my* chest isn't something I'd want anyone else but you to hear, sweetheart."

The endearment made Maggie's blood run cold, falling as it did into the quiet evening with all the fury and disgust of an obscenity.

CHAPTER NINE

BENNET stopped finally at a gazebo hidden from the rest of the house by a bank of rhododendrons that afforded him the privacy he so adamantly sought. Once there, he immediately let go of Maggie and, though he didn't exactly brush himself off, the way a person did when he accidentally got dirt on his clothes, he might as well have done.

"I believe congratulations are in order," he observed with silky contempt, rocking back on his heels and hooking his hands into his hip pockets. "The reluctant ex-wife of one of North America's wealthiest scions has successfully passed herself off as the simple Miss Jones, and made a royal fool of me into the bargain. I hope you found your charade amusing." He ran a cold, assessing glance over her. "Or did the reasons for your deception hinge on more material rewards, such as hooking another rich husband with your come-hither innocence, to replace the one you lost?"

His words stung like pellets of frozen rain but, of all his misconceptions, one in particular fixed itself in Maggie's mind. "*Reluctant* ex-wife?" She could barely contain an incredulous laugh. "Don't be absurd, Bennet! I was completely miserable married to Eric Carlson-Lewis."

"Which no doubt explains why you ran to him as fast as you could when you heard he was in Vancouver. Did you grovel very prettily when you saw him? Make your beautiful, deceitful eyes big and innocent? Flaunt a little flesh, perhaps, the way you did with me, to bait the trap?"

The wounds he inflicted would have felled her except that her outrage exceeded her hurt. "How dare you?" she whispered, shocked beyond measure at his capacity for cruelty. "How *dare* you smear what you and I shared with such hateful accusations? Not only are they the most insulting things anyone has ever said to me, they're also the most ridiculous! I wouldn't take Eric back if he were the last man on earth, and if you think for one moment that I would then you don't know me half as well as you think you do."

"I don't know you at all," Bennet shot back, in a cold, hard voice. "You're as much a fake as I thought your sapphires were when I first saw you wearing them tonight. But they're the real thing, aren't they?"

"Yes," Maggie retorted defiantly, "they're the real thing. Why does that upset you so much? Is it that you think lowly schoolteachers shouldn't be allowed such luxuries? That only the very gifted and elite members of society deserve such adornments?" She laughed again, scornfully this time. "If so, then I guess we're both fakes, Bennet. I didn't know you were such a snob."

Her retaliation snapped his control. "Don't try to sidetrack me with that sort of specious argument," he raged, flinging out both hands contemptuously. "For weeks—months, almost—you've represented yourself as someone you're not, prattling on about simple pleasures and integrity of personal values, and all the time you were just another woman who'd been bought off. When you told me you were divorced, talking about your marriage seemed to dredge up such unhappy memories that I felt sorry for you and wondered what sort of man would have let you go. Now I feel sorry for him. The only thing that makes you different from other women like you is that you charged a higher price."

He was unfair and unflattering, but most of all he was uninformed. "That is *not* true!"

"No? Your jewelry, all that priceless art and furniture that looks so absurdly out of place in your pathetic little house, are part of the payoff you exacted when your marriage fell apart. Isn't that the truth, Miss Jones—or would you prefer to be called Mrs. Carlson-Lewis?"

Maggie drew herself up to her full height and spoke very quietly and distinctly. "My name is Maggie Jones and I would prefer that you stop waving your arms about so imperiously. You're not conducting the New York Philharmonic now, Bennet Montgomery, and I'm not some cowering little second fiddle whose instrument is out of tune. I don't owe you any explanations, which doesn't mean I'm not willing to offer any, but I will not be shouted at and I will not be intimidated, so save the histrionics for someone who'll be impressed by them.''

She paused just long enough to snatch a breath. "Furthermore, I resent being called a liar. And as for having been 'bought off,' as you so charmingly phrase it, a few pieces of furniture and a couple of paintings were pitiful compensation for the mental and physical anguish I suffered as Eric Carlson-Lewis's wife. At the risk of sounding crass, I can tell you there wasn't enough money in the national coffers to persuade me that marriage to him, however brief, was worth the price.''

"Don't forget the sapphires," Bennet sneered.

"These sapphires were a gift from my dear and good friend, Wendy Carlson-Lewis, who happens also to be my former mother-in-law.''

"Well, how extraordinarily convenient! I suppose the fancy clothes were a gift, too?'' He reached out and tested the fabric of her gown appraisingly. "You're wearing a couple of thousand dollars' worth of merchandise on your back, tonight, Miss Jones, quite apart from the small fortune hanging around your neck. Don't tell me this outfit came out of your teacher's salary?''

"No, it didn't," she replied frankly, "and I'm not apologizing for it. This dress is one of several matrimonial leftovers, and before you accuse me of trying to keep them secret, too, let me point out what I'm sure would be obvious to you if you weren't in the throes of a tantrum: they're not exactly suitable garb for romping around your back garden or the beach in

Sagepointe, and that is why you haven't seen them before."

"Isn't it closer to the truth to say you were saving them for the right opportunity to—?"

"Don't interrupt until I'm finished! It was made abundantly clear to me, both by you and our hostess, that I was expected to dress up to the nines during my stay here, and all I've done is make sure I didn't disappoint either of you, so explain if you can why you're so angry. Pippa seemed quite delighted."

He glowered. "You know full well why."

"Yes, I do," she said boldly. "You wanted to play Professor Higgins to my Eliza Doolittle, and you can't stand it that I didn't need your guidance and patronage to climb to the top of the social heap. I haven't behaved like a grateful little ingénue of suitably humble origins, have I? Instead, I've turned out to be the ex-wife of someone you're afraid might outrank you on the social register, and whether or not that matters to me is irrelevant because it obviously matters so *damn* much to you!"

"It matters nothing to me," he said, turning away from her and tossing his words over his shoulder as though she were some vulgar stranger he couldn't wait to be rid of. "The people you know and how you care to exploit them is your own...affair."

He made the word "affair" sound incredibly sleazy. "I'm not sure what you're implying," she declared hotly, "but in case you're interested—"

"I'm not," he cut in, the words slashing at her. "Whatever makes you think I am?"

"We made love!"

Bennet wheeled around to face her then, and his smile was like a blast of winter slicing through the warm evening. "So we did," he agreed.

"Well, that meant something, Bennet, and I won't let you pretend that it didn't."

"Of course it meant something, Miss Jones. As you so perceptively observed, the first time it happened, I'm a normal man with all the normal urges. I'm not fool enough to turn away when opportunity presents itself." His lips thinned with distaste. "And neither, it turns out, are you, which explains your anxiety to sell yourself to the highest bidder. It's a pity your trip to Vancouver turned out to be such a waste of time."

Maggie stared at him, frustrated to seething point. Either he hadn't heard a single word she'd said, or else he preferred to believe gossip and hearsay from a stranger. He thought she'd sleep with him one night and someone else the next—including her detested ex-husband—if the price was right!

"However," Bennet continued, "I do like to maintain certain standards, one of them being never to settle for another man's leavings. It's not as though there aren't enough unattached women to go around, after all, and it's been my experience that married ladies in particular almost always create more problems than the pleasure of their company makes worthwhile."

"Don't they, though!" She almost spat the words at him. If he really believed what he was saying, then he was not the man she'd made him out to be, and she needed her head examined for almost falling in love with yet another jackass. Would she never learn? "That being the case, you'd no doubt like my resignation immediately?"

He condescended to look at her again then, and, whether or not it was a trick of the moonlight, Maggie didn't know, but his features seemed cast in marble and his eyes were bleak with disappointment. Maybe she was a beggar for punishment, or maybe she was just a fool, but a last flicker of hope refused to die. He was hurting, too, and why would he be, if he didn't care about her at least a little?

He covered it up quickly, though. "Not at all. I didn't hire you to benefit me. Christopher is doing well with you, and we both know how important it is for him to feel emotionally secure if his progress is to continue. You're a critical factor in his life at this point. He likes you and—" bitter amusement touched his mouth briefly "—he trusts you. For you to leave him now would be disastrous, especially since, starting almost immediately, my professional commitments will take me away from home on a regular basis. Most of my concert schedule is planned as much as three years in advance, and I'm not the sort of man who reneges on his contracts, any more than I'm content to leave rehearsals to an assistant director."

"You mean Christopher will have to manage without you for long periods of time?"

"For weeks, certainly. It's unavoidable."

"He'll be devastated!"

"I'm aware of that, Miss Jones, but he does have Mrs. Marshall, who's like a grandmother to him."

Bennet almost sighed, almost sounded regretful. "I once wondered, in what must surely have been a moment of madness, if perhaps you and I... Ah, well, it would have been a convenient arrangement at best, I suppose."

"What would have?"

"Nothing." He shot back his starched cuff and flicked a button that illuminated the dial of his watch. "We've wasted enough time on futile discussion already, and I'm sure our hostess is wondering what's keeping us."

"Just a minute, Bennet, I'm not finished."

"I am." Swinging away, he started back along the path to the house, leaving her to tag along behind or not, as she wished.

At that moment, Maggie didn't care that she prided herself on having become the kind of woman who'd never again beg for anything from a man, not even a few minutes of his time. She knew only that something fragile and breathtakingly beautiful hung in the balance, and she just couldn't stand idly by and let it get smashed to pieces without one more effort at saving it—not after that hint of regret for what might have been that she was sure she'd heard in his voice.

"I won't be dismissed this way," she told him and, when he ignored her and continued to walk away, she hiked up her long skirt and ran after him. "I won't, Bennet! This is too important."

She heard her voice tremble dangerously and felt the tears hot behind her eyes. "Why won't you listen to me?'' she pleaded, clutching his arm. ''Why won't you at least let me tell my side of the story?''

''Because you left it too late and I no longer care to know. It's none of my business.''

''Bennet,'' she pleaded, ''whatever else you choose to believe, you have to know that I stopped loving Eric years ago and that I never cared about his money. It got in the way of all the things that should have mattered more—things that I thought you and I shared, Bennet.''

But he was one of those men for whom there was only black or white, with no room in between for gray. She was not all that he'd hoped she was, and therefore was nothing that he wanted.

''Don't try to paint the nights we shared as anything other than what they really were,'' he advised her cruelly.

''And what was that?'' she couldn't help asking. When a woman's pride already lay in tatters, what more did she have to lose by hearing the whole truth?

''Two regrettable moments of impulse.''

''And they had nothing to do with love?''

He didn't so much as blink. ''Not a thing, and I'm surprised that a woman of your experience would even ask. I'd have thought you were more sophisticated than that.''

She could have tolerated anything but his indifference. It ripped apart all the excuses she'd been making not to accept what he'd been trying to tell her for the last half hour—that under no circumstances was he interested in a permanent involvement with her.

To give him credit, he'd guessed that, for her, things had taken a more serious turn, and he'd tried to let her down gently. She might view Eric's resurgence in her life as a disaster, but for Bennet it was obviously a godsend, an excuse to extricate himself from something that threatened to become an emotional burden. But did he also have to attack her integrity the way he had? Was he so embittered by the unhappy outcome of his engagement that he couldn't see that she was nothing like his former fiancée?

She got her answer soon enough. As though sensing he'd been unnecessarily harsh, he spoke more kindly. "We should have followed our first instincts, Maggie. You said at the outset that it was a mistake to try to mix business with pleasure, and you were right. As for myself, I have no excuses. I knew, right up to the moment I first kissed you on your front porch, that to allow things to progress any further was something I'd live to regret. It's just happened sooner rather than later, that's all, and for that we should be glad. At least no permanent harm's been done."

He lifted his hand as though he might touch her one last time, then changed his mind. "Stop looking for contentment in all the wrong places, Maggie. You were happy when we first met. Forget you ever knew me, go back to your simple farmers, and be happy again."

Her pride was not completely in ruins, after all. "Ranchers, Bennet," she corrected him icily, "and if you think, just because they get their hands dirty when they work, that they're ignorant country clods scraping a living from the land because it's all they're capable of doing, then you're even more misinformed than I thought. If snagging a rich husband was my chief priority, there are a few local men who'd qualify. Not only do they have more money than they can comfortably spend, but they're also enlightened enough to know appearances aren't important, that it's what's inside a person that counts, and that one rotten apple doesn't taint the whole barrel... which puts them light-years ahead of you. I could do a lot worse than set my cap at one of them."

This time he was the one left behind to trail after her or not, as he wished.

Somehow Maggie got through the next two days with the shell of her dignity intact. Somehow she presented a composed front when Bennet told her he would not be returning to Sagepointe with her and Chris, that he would be traveling, instead, to Vienna to preside over auditions for a televised Christmas concert he'd agreed to conduct the following year.

Somehow she brought Chris home, dealing with his boredom and fatigue, and taking late flights and picky Customs officials in her stride. Only when she arrived at the big house, on a hot, still day in late August, did she allow her facade to crack.

Consigning Chris to Mrs. Marshall's care, she took herself down the hall to the solarium and out through the glass doors to the patio. She huddled on the stone steps where the sun poured down, and waited for its heat to melt the cold spot that once had been her heart. Surely, when it did, she'd begin to feel again, and realize that her deep hurt stemmed entirely from having been unfairly tried and found guilty of crimes she hadn't committed, and against which she'd been offered no chance to defend herself?

Beau found her first. He came round the corner of the house and planted himself down beside her. He leaned against her, brave and strong and loyal, and she slid her arms around his neck and pressed her face against his soft, black fur, and let the misery run free.

He understood, turning his handsome head to lick at the tears that sprang up from the arid space inside and poured down her cheeks. The irony of it might have made her smile, once.

But that was just the beginning of the pain. The real agony took hold when Mrs. Marshall discovered her. The older woman sat down next to her, stuffed a tissue into her hand, then patted her shoulder. It was the most demonstrative gesture Maggie had ever known her to make to anyone.

"Well, missie," the housekeeper said, "I suppose Bennet's behind all this grieving and carrying on. I could see it coming a mile away."

"I've turned out to be a great disappointment to him," Maggie sniffed, mopping her tears and struggling to get a grip on herself.

Mrs. Marshall snorted. "You let yourself fall in love with him, and that was a big mistake. Worse yet, you tempted him, and now he's on the run."

"Fall in love with him?" Confronted by such certainty from someone else, Maggie backed away from the idea, nervous as a cat scenting danger. Not love, she thought. Love was treacherous, a deceiver, luring unwary victims into believing in miracles, then revealing itself to be nothing but wishful thinking fueled by lust. She wanted no part of it, especially not when all it seemed to generate was anger and mistrust. "Oh, no, I don't think so," she asserted.

Mrs. Marshall heaved herself to her feet. "Suit yourself, but I recognize the symptoms," she stated firmly. "You're letting him and the child, too, break your heart, Maggie, whether you want to admit it or not."

That was the whole problem, Maggie saw with belated clarity. She'd broken the first rule of self-preservation, and lost her objectivity. A man without a wife, a child without a mother, and a deep and unfulfilled need in herself had proved an irresistible combination. Somewhere along the way she'd slipped out of character. Instead of Miss Jones, the schoolteacher, she'd assumed the role of mother and started thinking of herself as a member of the Montgomery family. Worse yet, she'd shaped her emotions to suit the part.

Unfortunately, that wasn't an option Bennet had included in her contract, and the fact that he and she had become lovers merely complicated an already tangled situation. Yet, surely now that she'd recognized where she'd gone wrong, she could put her life back in order again, and, once she did, this awful, hollow sense of loss would go away.

Work. That was the answer. It had saved her before, and it would do so again. She would drive herself until she dropped. Strive for the impossible and accomplish it, beginning with Chris. Come hell or high water, that child was going to fit into the kindergarten class as well as anyone else, and be able to stay afloat without her, even if she had to work around the clock to devise ways to do it. Because, of course, she'd have to hand in her notice to take effect at Christmas, and she'd have to ask John Keyes to transfer her to another year in the meantime. She'd become too much the surrogate parent to be capable of assuming the role of impartial teacher, and, she suspected, too much the lover ever again to be merely an acquaintance. Some things were beyond even *her* mighty determination.

CHAPTER TEN

JOHN KEYES flung down Maggie's neatly typed letter of resignation. "I'm not accepting this," he declared flatly.

"But you have to," she said.

"Oh, no, I don't. You signed on for another year when you renewed your contract in May, and I'm not letting you off the hook that easily. It's tough enough getting teachers to work in remote places like this, without having to lose a good one like you for 'personal reasons.' Sorry, Maggie, but it just won't wash. You can have your transfer—Sally Best'll be glad to trade her rambunctious little grade four gang for your babies—but that's as far as I'll go."

She didn't need this. "John, I'm giving you almost four months in which to find a replacement. If I were sick, you'd have no choice."

"But you're not sick." He shot her a narrow glance. "It's got to do with that summer job at the big house, hasn't it? What's up? Is Montgomery giving you trouble?"

"We have our differences," she said evasively. "The situation—er—backfired."

"How so?"

"The details are personal and you don't really want to know about them."

But John wasn't the type to be easily deterred. He had the tenacity of an amiable bulldog, and a face to match. He didn't mind going after what he wanted, and where his school was concerned he wanted the best. "Yes, I do," he growled. "Be specific."

"I can't, John, so please don't ask. Can't you just accept that I've got to get away from here, and let it go at that?"

"No," he told her bluntly. "You're smart enough to know that running away never solved anything. You can chase halfway across the country and bury yourself in some town even smaller than this, but whatever it is that's really driving you away from here will go with you, and sooner or later you'll have to deal with it. Anyway," he finished slyly, "you got here first, so let him be the one to move on if you can't find happy-ever-after together."

She felt the color drain from her face. "I don't know what you're talking about."

John snorted, the way he was apt to do when dealing with particularly officious schoolboard trustees. "Do you want me to spell it out for you, Maggie?"

"No," she said hastily. She most emphatically did not wish to discuss Bennet. Thinking about him was painful enough.

John got up from his desk and went to look out over the school grounds that stopped just short of the lakeshore. "What about the boy? How do you think your leaving's going to affect him?"

"He'll adjust. The housekeeper's the most permanent part of his life, anyway. I'm only his tutor."

"You're a lot more than that, and we both know it. Can he sustain another loss at this stage of his life and not crawl back into his shell?"

Maggie had asked herself the same question, especially since learning that Bennet planned frequent absences, and didn't like the answers she kept coming up with. "I'm sure Mr. Montgomery would say that his nephew's mental well-being is his responsibility, not mine. Right from the start, he's made it clear I'm merely an employee."

"Then Mr. Montgomery's an even bigger fool than I thought." John swung back to search her face for a truth she might have overlooked. "Has it occurred to you, Maggie, that, by staying and seeing this thing through, the pair of you might find a way to work things out?"

What John didn't understand was that there was nothing to be worked out. Even if Mrs. Marshall had hit close to home with her assertion that Maggie had fallen in love with him, Bennet wasn't interested in trying to build a future on what he'd called "two regrettable moments of impulse."

She sighed. "I'm afraid that won't happen."

"For sure it won't, if you run away. You surprise me, you know. You never struck me as a quitter." He lifted his massive shoulders resignedly. "I guess none of us ever really knows what goes on inside someone else's head."

Or heart, not even one's own. She smiled wanly. "I guess not."

"Damn it, Maggie!" John's big hand slamming down on the desk had her almost jumping out of her skin. "Snap out of it! The role of tragedy queen doesn't suit you. You've got friends here, obligations. Don't let yourself be run out of a town that needs you as much as you need it. Montgomery's not going to be around that much longer. He told me when he first arrived that this is just a place to catch his breath. It's my guess he'll be moving on within the year and the big house will stand empty again. Who knows? He might even be gone by Christmas, and your resignation will have been for nothing."

He folded the letter and handed it back to her. "Take this and keep it—"

"John, no! I—"

"—for now. Another few weeks, one way or the other, isn't going to make any difference." A wry grin lit up his pleasantly ugly face. "Three months' notice is all you're required to give, anyway."

"I won't—"

"I know. You won't change your mind. My wife tells me the same thing all the time, then, when she changes it anyway, she tells me it's a woman's privilege." He slung an affectionate arm around Maggie's shoulders. "Sleep on it a while. Once term starts, you won't be running into Montgomery every day, and you might find things aren't quite as bad as you expected. And, for what it's worth, take Uncle John's advice and don't be so ready to throw in the towel. As someone once said, 'it ain't over 'til the fat lady sings.' ''

Maggie wrestled with his words for the rest of the day, even though she did her best to dismiss them. She knew that John was right. Running away never achieved anything. She could travel to the ends of the earth, but her heartache would stay with her.

"Okay," she told the fading petunias as she watered her garden that evening, "I'll get my life back on track the hard way. I'll stay."

After all, her work with Chris would come to an end when school started in another three weeks and, with someone else in charge of the kindergarten class, she wouldn't even have to see Bennet for the midterm parent-teacher interviews. As for the rest of the time, considering his aversion to mixing with local society, it ought to be a breeze. One thing she could count on—he wouldn't come seeking out her company again.

At first, she thought it was going to be easier than she'd expected. Whether at some level Chris sensed her unhappiness and, as children so often did, decided he was at fault and therefore tried harder than usual to please her, or whether the sudden change was a natural progression that would have occurred anyway, Maggie couldn't decide. All she knew was that his speech improved dramatically over the next little while. He relied less on gestures and started to accept full sentences as a normal mode of communication.

This brought to the surface a problem that had been festering for some time. Even before the trip down east, it had been obvious that he was growing bored with a routine he'd outgrown. Playing in the big, enclosed back garden no longer kept him happily occupied for hours. He was ready for broader horizons, and traveling had sparked in him a curiosity that demanded satisfaction.

It came as no great surprise to Maggie. She'd known from the outset that his social skills required interaction with other people, especially children, if they were to keep pace with the rest of his development. A bright child who was showing signs of reading readiness remained a handicapped child if he didn't know how to play and share with his peers. The difficulty had always been to convince Bennet of this.

He'd come back to town less than a week after she and Chris had arrived home, but she'd arranged things so that they saw very little of each other. To escape the heat of the late August days, she'd taken to conducting her classes with Chris down by the lake where it was cooler. She'd coax Mrs. Marshall into making up a picnic lunch, then she and Chris would set up house under his favorite willow tree, with Beau near by and more than eager to clean up any scraps. If Bennet continued to spy on them, at least Maggie wasn't aware.

Avoiding him completely, of course, was impossible, but when they did happen to meet she refused to linger in conversation. "Polite, pleasant and professional" became her motto. She wasn't about to give him reason to remind her again that she was being paid to work, not fraternize. The wounds he'd inflicted the night of Pippa's dinner party were still too fresh to bear further punishment.

He seemed strangely dismayed by her attitude. "For heaven's sake, Maggie," he'd scolded her once, "I'm not such a slave driver that you can't take a minute to tell me how you're doing."

He'd sounded almost as if he cared, but she'd refused to soften. That was how she'd gotten into trouble with him in the first place. "It won't take a minute to tell you. I've never been better," she'd replied shortly, then hurried off to find whatever it was she'd come looking for, aware that his gaze followed her in that smoldering way that unsettled her so.

Now she was going to have to search him out deliberately and try once more to convince him to let her take Chris into Sagepointe and "parade him through town." Before the trip to New York, he'd still been firmly opposed to the idea. "It isn't necessary. He already gets out," he'd said defensively. "He spends every Saturday morning around other people."

She knew that was true. Seldom a Monday had gone by that she hadn't noticed Chris had something new: toys, perhaps, or clothes, or even just a haircut. But that was before, when most of the summer had stretched ahead. Very soon now, the child was going to have to deal with a class full of strangers, and if Bennet thought visiting a shopping mall in Annisville once a week, or a few days in Manhattan and Long Island, as suitable preparation for an only child about to begin his formal education in Sagepointe, then she had news for him. It was time Chris saw the school he'd be attending, and met Sally Best, his teacher. It was past time for him to gain firsthand knowledge of the town in which he lived.

Maggie dreaded the thought of having to approach Bennet. As long as he remained out of sight, so did the hurting. But face-to-face with him again, all the pain came rushing to the surface and she was terribly afraid that she'd forget what it was she'd originally planned to ask for, and end up begging for things he wouldn't give her.

As it happened, she worried for nothing. "He caught the early flight from Vancouver to Toronto," Mrs. Marshall informed her, when Maggie, unable to find him anywhere else, ended up looking for him in the kitchen. "A big recording session, as I understand. If it goes well, he might be back for the weekend, but he said not to expect him. An old friend of his has a place out at one of the lakes, and he usually spends a few days with her if he can spare the time."

Maggie felt as if she'd been landed a blow to her midsection. There was a "her" in his life! Was *she* the real reason he regretted having jumped into bed with the local schoolteacher?

Mrs. Marshall stopped rolling out the pastry she'd been making for a peach pie, and looked at her. "Why don't you come straight out and ask who she is, missie, instead of standing there turning green about the gills and trying to pretend you don't care?"

"Because I don't," Maggie insisted, struggling to regain control of her emotions. "It's none of my business."

The housekeeper huffed with exasperation and ignored the reply. "She's a retired pianist who played at his first concert, though why I'm telling you, since you're so sure you don't care, I can't imagine. Maybe it's because I can see what's as plain as the nose on yonder dog's face, if only you weren't too stubborn to take a look."

It was time to change the subject. "Did Mr. Montgomery leave any special instructions for Chris before he left?"

"Not a one." The housekeeper resumed rolling out her pastry. "He knows the boy's in good hands."

The gods, Maggie decided, were on her side, for a change. "Then I'll just go ahead with the next phase of instruction. We won't be needing lunch today, Mrs. Marshall. We're going out."

The rolling pin swiveled to a halt once more. "Well, now, he didn't say anything about *that*, and we both know how he feels on the subject."

"I'll take full responsibility," Maggie said with more confidence than she really felt. "I'm just taking Chris down to get acquainted with the school, beforehand. Mr. Montgomery knows it's something that has to be done. We've talked about it already." He just doesn't know when, and, by the time he finds out, there won't be much he can do about it!

She collected Chris, slipped a leash on Beau's collar, and whisked them down the driveway and out to the road before Mrs. Marshall had time to raise further objection or make anymore astute observations on the true state of Maggie's heart. "It's a special treat," she told an excited Chris, "because you've been such a good boy and worked so hard."

They had a wonderful morning, stopping by the park to play on the swings, then visiting the school, where Maggie showed Chris his classroom and let him draw with chalk on the blackboard. Finally, they ended up at Sagepointe's only fast-food restaurant, where they sat outside at a plastic table to which they tied the end of Beau's leash. They ate hamburgers and french fries covered with catsup, and Chris discovered the joy of slurping a chocolate milkshake through a straw.

The next day he drew a picture of their outing. It wasn't great art—Maggie's hair resembled a sulphur yellow bird's nest and Beau's legs were so long, he looked more horse than dog—but it was the most creative drawing Chris had produced so far, and justified her decision to bend the rules a bit. The child was thirsty for new experiences, soaking them up like a sponge.

Mrs. Marshall was suitably impressed. "Why, if that's not wonderful!" she said, and made the day complete for Chris by taping the drawing to the door of the refrigerator.

The next few days followed a similar pattern of success. By Thursday, Chris knew his way to school, could find his classroom by himself, and had made tentative overtures of friendship with a couple of other children his age. One morning, Sally Best had spent half an hour getting to know him, and all the way home he'd bragged about his new teacher, leaving Maggie to repress the jealousy that boiled up inside her at the thought of another woman supplanting her in his affections.

On Friday, everything fell apart. The day started out to be the same as all the others, except that it rained in the morning so they postponed their outing until the afternoon. Then, just for a change, Maggie decided they'd follow the path along the lakefront instead of walking along the road.

Blackberries, washed clean by the rain, hung from the bushes in glistening clusters. Soon Chris's face and the front of his T-shirt were stained purple with juice, and his eyes sparkled with glee at this latest adventure. Beau, unhampered by the leash for once, and equally ecstatic, raced along the sandy beach, dashing into the water every now and then in hopeless pursuit of birds.

As usual, once they arrived at the school Maggie tied the dog to the bicycle rack and left Chris happily climbing on the bars of the jungle gym, while she went inside the building to check the resource center for tapes and videos that would help her with her new curriculum. She knew well enough that a poorly prepared teacher ended up with a rowdy class, and, in her present state of mind, waging a discipline battle five days a week on top of everything else was more than she was prepared to cope with.

The information she sought was stored on microfiche, and it wasn't often that the one computer monitor available for use in the school stood idle. That last Friday afternoon in August, though, no one else was waiting to use it.

She'd intended to take only a short time, fifteen minutes at the most. A glance from the window before she started told her that Chris was perfectly content. Even though there weren't any other children to keep him company that day, enough school personnel were about the place to reassure her that he wasn't really alone. They all knew who he was and something of his history, and Maggie judged that he was safe enough playing by himself for a little while.

But somehow time slipped by without her noticing, and it took the oppressive sound of silence filtering into her consciousness to raise the first prickle of alarm. A glance at her watch showed that almost an hour had gone by, and she had no idea how long it had been since she'd stopped being aware of other people coming and going.

Leaving her notes and briefcase scattered over the table, Maggie ran down the long hall toward the front entrance. Beyond the double doors the sun shone reassuringly and the trees shimmered in the heat. But the playground stood ominously empty. Only Beau, ears erect and gaze fixed unwaveringly on the path to the beach, told her in which direction to start looking for Chris.

"Don't panic," she muttered to the dog, whose impatience to be free to go searching for the child hampered her efforts to untie him. "We'll find him playing in the sand, or eating berries. We will!"

But all they found were the sneakers Chris had been wearing, soaking wet and abandoned at the water's edge a few yards along the beach path. The fear Maggie had tried to tame ran wild then, a bitter, choking taste in her mouth, and the next thing she knew she was knee-deep in the lake, her skirt clinging to her legs and Beau thrashing along beside her. She screamed Chris's name over and over, and the placid lake flung it back at her in mocking, empty echoes.

He's not here, vanishing sanity told her. The water's shallow, you'd see him. He was wearing a white shirt and red shorts.

But children could drown in two inches of water, and the sun, blazing down on the lake's surface, blinded her to everything but her own fear. Reason had no place in the dread that seeped through her, sucking away all the warmth.

Suddenly she didn't want to see, didn't want to know. All that mattered was that she get out of the water fast, in case a lifeless little hand wrapped itself around her submerged ankles, or that angelic face floated up—

"No!" Her cry fractured the nightmare, and she became aware of Beau tugging her away, angling back toward the shore, his black fur sleek against his ribs and his ears flattened against his skull.

"What?" she whispered, terrified, convinced his keener eyesight had detected something she'd missed. "What is it, Beau?"

Whining softly, he turned his head to look at her, his eyes alive with intelligence. When she didn't respond, he stopped pretending that she was in charge, and set off for the house, half a mile further along the path, with her following behind on the other end of his leash.

The french doors to the living room stood wide open. As she raced the last few yards across the terrace, she could hear voices, a woman's sharp and eager blending with the deeper tones of a man's. And then Beau was across the threshold, dragging her behind like a piece of limp rag, and there was Bennet, a monolith of grave displeasure.

"Bennet!" A great, shuddering sigh escaped as a sob, and she reached out for him. "Chris—I can't— oh, Bennet, I thought he was—the water's not very deep, but I couldn't find him and I looked, Bennet, I went right in and he wasn't there and I—"

The words tumbled out, incoherent and frantic between the dry, ragged sobs, and she was pawing at Bennet, clutching at his arms, trying to shake him into action because he wasn't hearing her. He wasn't understanding. He was taking her hands and holding them away from him, and speaking over his shoulder, his face a mask of annoyance.

She was behaving badly, creating a scene, and there was someone else in the room—not Mrs. Marshall, who should have been there, bringing in tea and the little iced cookies that Chris loved, but Edith Caverley, who would tell everyone in town that Bennet Montgomery's nephew had drowned and it was all

Maggie Jones's fault for having disobeyed the rules. No wonder Bennet was annoyed.

Maggie saw his mouth moving, felt his hands pushing her down, their pressure causing her knees to give way. The floor came up to meet her, but somehow the couch caught her instead, and Bennet turned away, not seeming to care that her wet skirt would leave stains all over his elegant silk upholstery.

Edith Caverley's face hovered. "... picking berries to make jam and minding my own business, I'm sure," she said, and she sounded terribly offended "... thought I was doing you a favor... didn't think you'd want him wandering down there by himself."

Then Bennet was back, bending down and holding a glass to Maggie's mouth and pouring poison down her throat. "We're very grateful," he said over his shoulder. "Do you mind seeing yourself out? I need to take care of Miss Jones."

He was going to kill her, which was what she deserved, Maggie thought, choking furiously as the liquid burned the last scrap of air out of her lungs.

But his hands, smoothing the hair away from her face, were gentle, and his voice, when he spoke to her, was kind. "Take it slowly," he told her, then, when she did and was able to breathe again, he brought the glass back to her lips and said, "Finish the rest of it now. You look like death warmed up."

That was when the tears started. The grief poured out of her, streaming down her cheeks, a silent flood that contorted her face and made her as ugly outside as she felt within. It was as if everything that gave her substance was melting into one long, endless river of combined sorrows. All that kept her from being swept away was Bennet's arms holding her against him, and the steady beat of his heart.

Gradually reason inched back and brought control with it. She was able to hear the words Bennet spoke, and comprehend their meaning. "Chris is safe, Maggie. Mrs. Marshall's taken him upstairs to change his clothes. He's covered in sand and blackberry juice."

She tried to speak, and heard her question emerge as a croak. "How?"

"Your neighbor found him picking berries on the beach path. She thought he'd wandered away from the house, and brought him home."

"I found his shoes," Maggie said, her throat raw all over again. "I thought—"

"We wondered where they were. I guess they got wet, so he kicked them off."

"Why didn't she bring him back to the school?"

"She didn't know you were there, and I gather he wouldn't talk to her when she asked him why he was alone. You know how he is with strangers."

She wished he'd lose his temper, wished he'd come right out and tell her she was an irresponsible fool not fit to be let loose around children. She could stand anything but the tender way he had her wrapped in his arms, as if he held himself more to blame than her.

"I'm so sorry, Bennet," she whispered, burying her face against him, afraid that if she looked into his eyes she'd see the disappointment and betrayal he must surely feel.

"I know," he said, and for a moment she thought she felt his lips in her hair. There was such comfort in the breadth of his shoulders, such a feeling of security in his arms.

"Is he strong enough that he dares to be kind?" Wendy had asked that day they'd met for lunch and Maggie had told her about Bennet. It seemed a lifetime ago, and she'd thought she knew the answer then, but only now, without the memory of passion to cloud the issue, did she fully appreciate the depth of integrity and gentleness that were the true source of his strength.

She would have stayed in his arms forever if she could, but already he was pulling away. "Well," she muttered, sitting up straighter and wiping her face dry with the heel of her hand, "I suppose I have to try to justify why I deliberately went against your wishes."

"I think I know why," Bennet said.

"It wasn't that I wanted to defy you, Bennet. I truly believed it was time—school starts the week after next, and he had to—"

"I know. Stop blaming yourself. It's as much my fault as anyone's. I'm beginning to realize that the only way any of us survives and grows is by learning to face up to the way things really are. He can't go through life with a guard dog in tow to make sure he stays safe. It's our job to teach him to do that for himself."

"But I left him alone, and I'm supposed to know better. Children his age . . . they don't have a very long attention span, and I'd already seen how quickly he was becoming bored, lately." Maggie heard the quaver in her voice, saw again in her mind the glassy, empty surface of the lake, and covered her eyes despairingly. "He could have drowned, Bennet, and it would have been all my fault."

"It would have been my fault as well," he corrected her, and slid his arms around her again. "It's time I accepted that the world's not perfectly safe and life's not perfectly designed to measure up to my expectations, Maggie. This house sits by the lake, the school is next to the lake. The whole town is situated on the lake, for heaven's sake, and pretending otherwise isn't going to change any of it. I'm the one who has to adapt and teach Chris to respect the water in the same way that he has to respect traffic. If all the other children in town can learn, then so can he."

"But Chris is different."

"Not really. I've insisted that everyone treat him as if he's different, which was a mistake. Underneath he's just an ordinary kid who got off to a lousy start. Now that he's catching up with the rest of the herd, he's going to get dirty, scrape his knees, break rules, and probably come home with a black eye or two." Silent laughter rumbled through him. "It's the nature of the male animal, Maggie, and we've got to accept that and teach him to survive anyway because, if we don't, the worry and the stress are going to kill us both."

We? Us? This wasn't the Bennet she knew, saying these things to her. Something had blunted the hard edges of his certainty. Instead of rebuffing her, he was drawing her to him, smoothing her hair, touching her face, and cupping both hands around her jaw as though he wanted to kiss her. His eyes were a soft and hazy gray behind their veil of lashes, and overflowing with an emotion that had more to do with love than reproach.

"Maggie…" he began, and his voice was like gravel resisting the undertow of a gentle wave. "Maggie, I've had a lot of time to think and…well, I wonder if—"

The phone rang once, twice, three times. He rested his forehead against hers and closed his eyes. "Damn!" he muttered softly. "I'd forgotten I was expecting a call. Do you suppose, if I ignore it, my agent will think I've not yet arrived home?"

"He might." Maggie dared to let her fingers sift through his hair.

But the caller was persistent. The ringing went on until finally, and with undisguised impatience, Bennet let her go and crossed the room to snatch up the receiver. "Yes, Norman? Do you have the new audition dates?"

Maggie sat scarcely daring to hope, wishing that Bennet had had time to finish what he'd started to say to her before the phone had interrupted. Had his feelings for her really undergone change, or was her overstimulated imagination misleading her into reading more into his words and actions than he intended?

"Yes," he said again to the caller, and this time his tone held something more than impatience. Maggie looked up from smoothing out the creases in her damp skirt to find him staring at her, the expression on his face carefully blank, and it was as though a chill rippled up her spine. "Yes, she's here."

He held out the phone to her. "It's your ex-husband," he said tonelessly. "He wants to speak to you."

Her brain seemed incapable of absorbing yet another shock. "No," she protested, huddling farther into the corner of the couch. "No, it can't be him. He doesn't have this number."

"Apparently, he does." Bennet gestured again with the telephone, his eyes remote.

She had no choice but to obey his silent summons, but she handled the receiver as if it were a loaded gun. "Don't go," she begged as he moved toward the door. "I have nothing to say to Eric that you can't hear."

Just briefly, Bennet hesitated, then shrugged. "If you say so."

"I do," she whispered, then spoke directly into the mouthpiece, spitting out the words as if they were bullets. "What's going on, Eric, and how did you get this number?"

"Sorry if I called at an inopportune time, dear Margaret."

He sounded so close she could almost see the sneer on his face. "Just answer my question," she snapped, her eyes swinging anxiously to Bennet. He stood at the window, trying to appear relaxed, but his posture was as rigid as a soldier's on parade.

"My mother had another heart attack this morning."

"What?" She gripped the phone tightly, unwilling to believe what she was hearing. Wendy was getting better, not worse. She was due to be discharged from the hospital soon, and planned to convalesce in Arizona. "How bad is it?"

"They've managed to stabilize her, but it doesn't look good, Margaret. Her heart sustained considerable damage and she could have another attack any time."

Maggie sagged, the energy that had carried her this far draining away at this latest piece of news. What the gods gave with one hand they took away with another, it seemed. "But she was doing so well. What happened?"

"Don't ask me. You know what these hospitals are like. No one tells you anything." The petulance with which she was so familiar crept into Eric's voice. "Look, I'm supposed to let you know that she's asking for you, though why she needs you when she has her husband and son at her bedside is beyond me."

"I'll be there as soon as I can. Please tell her that, and also that I love her."

After the connection was broken, Maggie stood for a minute, leaning with both hands on the table, knowing that Bennet had turned and was watching her, waiting for her to speak. "Wendy had another heart attack. I have to go to her, Bennet," she said at last. "I don't want to. I wish I could stay here, that we could finish whatever it was we started, but I have to live with myself. And that means I have to go, whether or not you understand, whether or not you like it."

CHAPTER ELEVEN

BENNET didn't argue, which should have made Maggie grateful, but in fact left her only more unhappy. "You'll need to change your clothes," he said, and rummaged in his pockets for the keys to his car. "I'll take you home. It will save time."

"Thank you."

Too soon, they were pulling up before her house. "I'll be back in an hour to drive you into the city," he told her. "Try to be ready."

For what? she wondered, and wished he'd say something more, touch her, give her something to nourish her tiny hopes and sustain her through what lay ahead.

But all he said was, "Hurry," and leaned across her to swing open the car door and speed her on her way.

She showered and changed, then packed a bag, too dazed to think logically about what she'd need. A toothbrush, of course, and extra clothes, because she'd have to stay until things were settled, one way or another. And credit cards, since she had only about fifteen dollars in her purse.

She ran back downstairs, swept up the day's mail that sat unopened on her desk, stuffed it in the side pocket of her overnight bag, and was halfway down

the steps leading from the porch when Bennet's car
pulled up.

"Get in," he ordered, taking her bag and slinging
it in the back seat.

"You don't have to go with me, you know," she
said, tempting fate to dash her budding hopes before
they reached full bloom. "I've got my own car. I can
drive myself."

"Do as you're told for a change, Maggie," he replied briefly. "The state you're in, you'd probably
wind up in the ditch. I'll do the driving, deliver you
safely to the hospital, and find you a place to stay.
You've got enough on your mind without having to
worry about things like that."

It was so much what she wanted to hear that, at
first, she didn't think to question the wisdom of his
actions. Yet, as the miles slid by, the consequences of
what having him by her side might entail, once they
arrived in Vancouver, loomed larger in her mind.
"You know, Bennet," she began, sneaking a look at
him, "this might not be such a good idea."

He spared her a quick glance. "What are you talking about?"

"Your being there—" she waved a vague hand at
the western horizon "—in the city, with me."

"I was going to drive in later this evening anyway.
Tomorrow morning I'm flying to Boston for a couple
of days, then going on to London. Things I neglected
over the summer—auditions, promotions, media interviews, and stuff like that—are starting to pile up,
and can't be put off any longer." The sun slipped be-

hind the hills, reducing the vicious glare. Steering with one-handed expertise, Bennet removed his sunglasses and tucked them into the console that separated the front seats. "And besides, my car is faster and I'm probably a better driver. We'll be there sooner this way."

Getting there wasn't what concerned her. It was what was waiting for them at the other end that mattered: Eric's unpredictable spite that she knew could rise above any other consideration—even one as fraught with potential tragedy as this—and the undimmed pleasure he'd always taken in setting her at a disadvantage.

The day he'd found her visiting Wendy had taught Maggie the folly of hoping that time might soften his hostility toward her. She'd had the temerity to divorce him, and she realized now that that was not something he'd ever forgive. Nobody rejected Eric Carlson-Lewis, especially not before the whole world.

She tried again. "Eric will be there. It might be better if he didn't know you were with me."

"I'm not interested in what's best for him," Bennet informed her. "It's your relationship with his mother that prompted me to get involved."

It wasn't so much what he said as how he said it that opened up the chasm between them. Suddenly they were on opposite sides again, and she didn't have the first idea how to bridge the distance that separated them. They might have been traveling parallel routes through space, carried on the twin beams of the headlights cutting through the late summer dusk. Co-

cooned in the soft touch and expensive smell of leather, Maggie ought to have felt safe, cared for. Instead she felt as if she were speeding alone toward such total destruction that not even her most private dreams could survive.

Eric was the first person they saw as they entered the waiting area outside the coronary care unit at the hospital. His silk suit looked a little rumpled and his hair was not arranged quite carefully enough to hide its thinning condition.

"You took your time getting here," he greeted them.

"As a matter of fact," Bennet retorted, "we made remarkably fast time. How is your mother?"

Eric's pale eyes, which had settled fleetingly on Maggie, fastened on Bennet. "Margaret," he said, "who is this man?"

Only Eric, Maggie thought with sinking dread, could imbue such a simple question with so much insult. Stunningly aware of Bennet at her side, sudden tension radiating from him in waves, and of the expectant silence that followed Eric's question, she cleared her throat. "This is Mr. Bennet Montgomery, my employer," she said, and heard the conciliation in her tone.

Bennet heard it, too. For no more than a heartbeat his eyes probed past her features, as though trying to determine what motivated her need to placate a man she'd sworn she despised.

I'm trying not to do or say anything that will give him reason to create a scene, she wanted to explain. Things are already fragile enough between you and me. I don't want him offending you with innuendoes.

But she saw the way Eric's mouth snapped shut and a muscle in his jaw danced with sudden rage, and she knew that, whatever Bennet might have deduced from her reply, she had not deceived Eric. He knew her too well, and that uncanny intuition which he'd used so ruthlessly to manipulate her in the past told him now that Bennet Montgomery was much more than her employer.

It was the straw that broke Maggie's back. Without warning, the shell of her composure crumpled. She didn't need a mirror to tell her that she'd grown pale under her tan and that her hands were shaking.

Moving with the speed he characteristically employed whenever he set out to intimidate a person, Eric strode across the floor and came to a halt so close to her that his tobacco-stale breath fanned her face.

"How dare you?" he snarled. "My mother is hanging on to life by a thread because she wants to see you again before she dies, and you—" his hand shot out and she felt his fingers close viciously around her wrist, crushing the fine bones until she almost cried out "—you have the gall to show up here with your lover in tow."

"No!" she began. "He's—"

Without seeming to move, Bennet insinuated himself between them. "Take your hand off her," he ordered, his voice ominously soft.

Eric's head swung to Bennet in slow motion. "And if I choose not to?"

Bennet's smile was tight and dangerous. "Then I'll break your arm."

He spoke with such deadly sincerity that Maggie believed him. So, apparently, did Eric. He cast a nervous eye around. "Perhaps you don't know who it is you're threatening," he blustered.

Bennet didn't so much as blink. "Perhaps I don't care," he said, and Eric's fingers slackened and released her.

Maggie felt Bennet's hand in the small of her back, encouraging her toward the swinging doors. "Go see your mother-in-law, Maggie, and when you're ready to leave meet me in the lobby downstairs."

Although she'd had no experience with death, Maggie knew the moment she set eyes on her that Wendy was going to die. There was a transparency to her, as though part of her was already gone. Only her eyes were still alive.

"Darling," she breathed, "I waited for you to come."

Maggie reached for the hand that was too weak to do more than flutter in her direction. "I came as soon as I heard and I'm not leaving until you promise to get better."

"No promises, darling, not this time."

The words hung on little puffs of air, so fragile that Maggie had to bend close to hear them. "Don't talk like that," she said, blinking fiercely to keep the tears in check. "Don't you know this is the age of medical miracles? You aren't allowed to give up."

Wendy's smile was almost ethereal. "Some lives," she said, "aren't worth fighting for." Her eyes drifted to the window, beyond which floodlights glowed on a roofgarden full of potted geraniums. "So many regrets and no strength to erase them. But you—" her gaze came back to rest lovingly on Maggie's face "—you, my darling child, are one of my brightest memories. I cannot believe there was a time when I didn't know you and love you."

The world had been spinning out of control for days, events piling up one on top of another with perilous disregard for the laws of gravity. Suddenly the weight tilted and it was more than Maggie could do to stem the avalanche of despair that threatened to bury her. "Don't die!" she heard herself beg, the tears streaming openly down her face.

It was the wrong thing to say. She had no business asking anything of this dear, dear woman, especially not now. But to lose her was unthinkable, something so unbearably painful and cruel that she couldn't stand it.

Eric's voice hissed in her ear. "Get out of here if you can't control yourself, Margaret, and don't bother to come back because you won't be allowed in! My mother's in no condition to deal with your hysteria."

She stumbled from the room, blinded with grief.

As he'd promised, Bennet was waiting in the main lobby. He came to her, a tall, dark silhouette blurred by the tears she seemed unable to stem.

"I'm so sorry, Maggie."

She felt as if, one by one, she was losing all the people who mattered most—first Bennet, then through him, Christopher, and now Wendy. Directly or otherwise, Eric had poisoned her relationship with each of them. "She's my best friend, and he's forbidden me to see her again," Maggie said, not caring that her voice, and the words themselves, sounded as plaintive as a child's. "He always predicted that I'd pay for walking out on him, and now he's seeing to it that I do."

Bennet slid a consoling arm around her shoulder. "Never mind him."

But she couldn't hold back the memories. "We were outside the courtroom, right after the divorce," she recalled, the chilling venom of the man she'd once thought she loved resurrected with powerful clarity by her most recent exposure to him. "He said, 'I wish you every bad thing that can happen to a person. I hope you're miserable for the rest of your life and that—'"

"I wish I'd waited for you upstairs," Bennet muttered, "but then again, it's well I didn't. The temptation to rearrange your ex-husband's expensively capped teeth would have proved irresistible. Let's get out of here, Maggie."

She felt like Alice, trapped in a dream. Nothing had substance. The walls of the building undulated back and forth, one minute about to close in on her, the next receding a vast distance. The flight of steps outside the main entrance to the hospital seemed as steep as a mountain. She inched down tentatively, because her feet no longer obeyed the commands her brain was sending to them.

"Are you going to faint on me, Maggie?"

His voice, his strength, the aura of power he wore so naturally, partially revived her. "Certainly not. I'm not the fainting type," she said, but her voice lacked its usual vitality. She sounded as limp as a dishrag.

He was studying her, unconvinced. "Then let's go."

She pulled away from him. "I can't leave. What if Wendy—? I want to be close by, in case—"

"You will be," he assured her, reaching for her arm again and guiding her the rest of the way down the steps. "And I promise that you'll be allowed to see her again, if that is what both you and she wish."

Maggie believed him because she had nothing else to cling to. "Where are we going?"

"I've booked you into the hotel I always use when I stay in town. It's a ten-minute taxi ride away, it's quiet and comfortable, and it has a passably good restaurant." He traced a finger under her eyes. She could only imagine how puffy and unattractive they must look with all the crying they'd done. "When did you last eat?"

"I don't remember."

He shook his head reprovingly, the way she'd so often seen him do with Chris. "Shame on you, Miss Jones! You ought to know better."

The "quiet, comfortable hotel" was luxurious. Her room on the tenth floor faced west, overlooking a private marina and beyond to the darker waters of Georgia Strait.

"I'm just across the hall," Bennet told her, depositing her overnight bag on the luggage stand and dropping her room key on the top of the television set. "The restaurant doesn't close for another half hour. Wash your face and meet me in five minutes, then we'll go and eat."

The "passable restaurant" was supervised by a Swiss chef; the food was superb. Certain she was too tired and worried to have any appreciation for what she ate, Maggie found herself suddenly ravenous as a platter of assorted hors d'oeuvres was set on the table. There was smoked salmon and capers, marinated calamari, and fat olives bursting with Greek sunshine. There were tiny fresh oysters on the half shell and triangles of melba toast heaped with caviar.

"I thought we'd share those," Bennet remarked with dry amusement.

Unrepentant, Maggie realized she'd eaten the lion's share while he'd been content with a glass of chardonnay. "I'm not fond of olives," she allowed, pushing the platter toward him.

The laugh she'd always loved burst out. "You're too generous, Miss Jones! I hope you left room for your steak."

She had thought nothing could make her smile again, at least not that day, but when Bennet Montgomery set out to be charming there was no resisting him. Dinner became an occasion.

He teased her through the salad course, toasted her with cabernet over the steaks, regaled her with tales of his travels and work, and, when she hesitated over the dessert trolley, he made the choice for her and selected a white chocolate mousse that would have had a dietician throwing up her hands in despair.

Ignoring her protests, he told the waiter, "We'll have brandy with our coffee."

"Are you trying to make me tipsy?" she asked, leaning back in her chair and smiling.

"I'm trying to get you to relax," he said, and the laughter was gone suddenly from his voice. "I think there are going to be some difficult days ahead for you, and you're going to need all the strength you can command to deal with them." He swirled his brandy once and looked into its depths as though he searched for a solution to her problems. "I gather that your ex-husband resents you being close to his mother."

"Yes," Maggie confirmed dully. The mere mention of Eric's name was enough to snuff out the temporary respite from anxiety that she'd enjoyed over dinner. "If he won't let me see her again, it might be better for me to go home."

"If she asks to see you," Bennet said, "there's nothing he can do to stop you from visiting. In view of her condition, it seems to me that you have every right to remain within call if that's what you wish to do."

Maggie sighed, the weariness she'd shoved aside sweeping back all at once and making everything look bleak again. "He can make things very unpleasant."

"Only if you let him, Maggie." Bennet's glance was very direct. "And you'll let him only if he still matters to you."

Her look was every bit as candid. "He doesn't matter to me, Bennet," she said with quiet certainty. "He hasn't mattered to me for a very long time. If Wendy—" She bit her lip to stop it from trembling. The wine and brandy had taken their toll; she was at the mercy of her emotions. She tried again. "If Wendy dies—and I'm afraid she will because she's lost the will to live—my one consolation will be that I'll have no reason to see him or speak to him ever again."

Bennet studied his empty snifter. "Do you hate him?"

"No," she replied unhesitatingly. "Hate is a very powerful thing, and I can't be bothered wasting my energy on it where he's concerned. If I feel anything at all when I see him, it's..."

Revulsion that he ever touched me!

Bennet looked up, catching her off guard. "What?" he asked sharply. "Finish what you were going to say."

"Regret," she improvised, and saw at once that she'd made a mistake.

His expression darkened. "Why?" he asked, and she knew that all the doubts he'd once expressed about her were rising to the surface again. Even after everything he'd witnessed at the hospital, he still questioned her integrity. What would it take to convince him differently?

"Because you weren't my first lover," she admitted, desperation making her rash, "and when I remember that *he* was, I feel defiled."

At first, she thought she'd pushed him too far. His eyes glowed like coals, then, "Finish your brandy," he ordered abruptly, flinging down his napkin and pushing back his chair. "This isn't the place to get into all that."

There was an inner courtyard in the hotel, where a fountain splashed and tropical bougainvillea flowered in huge clay pots. "We can walk here a while," Bennet said, steering her through paned glass doors, "or we can go upstairs, to your room or mine."

"Here," she said, not trusting herself, or him.

The decorous hand he'd placed at her back as they'd left the dining room slid to the nape of her neck and was not decorous at all. "Maggie," he began, swinging to face her and blocking out the light spilling through the windows from the chandelier in the foyer, "you once asked me if sex had anything to do with love."

"And you said no."

He lowered his head, and his mouth touched hers in a kiss that began as brief but forgot to end. He tasted of brandy, smelled of sandalwood. He felt... oh, he felt *right*! As if his were the only arms that should hold her, his the only body that should shield her, bring her joy, give her love. She knew at that moment that there would never be anyone else like him, that he was the only man she wanted in her life.

"What would you say," he murmured, his hands framing her face, "if I told you I'm no longer so sure I was right? That, where you and I are concerned, it's become less a matter of not trusting you than of not being sure I can trust myself?"

The soft thunder of desire rolled between them. How easy it would be to let it deafen her to reason, to settle for a little and try to make it last a lifetime. Only the knowledge of how lonely and uncertain all her tomorrows might be gave Maggie the strength to resist. He had doubts. She could hear them in his voice now, she'd seen them in his eyes as recently as half an hour ago.

She slid her mouth free. "I'd say ask me again when you are sure," she replied breathlessly.

"I'm a selfish man, Maggie, unused to sharing myself with others. My work has always come first.

"It's been hard, adjusting to having a child intrude in my life, but knowing he has other people to turn to, like you and Mrs. Marshall, gives me the freedom to pursue my career. But with a woman like you—" his eyes roamed her face searchingly "—I find myself thinking about settling down in one place, of being the one to give you the things you were meant to have—a home, a husband, children—and I don't know if I *can* give you all that without losing my identity. It could take me some time to find out. Do you have the patience and courage to wait?"

"I don't know," she replied honestly. How could she answer truthfully when he was so uncertain? She could wait for years, loving him more with every passing day, and at the end of it all he might still walk away from her.

He groaned and held her tighter. "Why don't you ever make things easy for me, Miss Jones? Right now I want you so much, I'm ready to sell my soul for you. I want to say, Let's seize tonight and to hell with tomorrow, but I think we both know that, in the long run, that's not the route to take."

It was absurd to feel so let down. "Precisely," she said, her voice as dry as an old prune. "Liquor loosens one's inhibitions dreadfully, doesn't it?"

She felt him sag against her, then a slow rumble of laughter fought its way up from the depths of his chest. "Dear Miss Jones," he said, releasing her all but for one hand which he kept trapped in his, "you have such a way with words!"

He walked her back inside and didn't speak again until they reached her door. "I probably won't see you in the morning," he said, leaning against the wall and winding a stray lock of her hair around one finger. "I have a very early flight. Stay here as long you feel you must, and don't worry about Chris. Mrs. Marshall will take good care of him. Don't worry about the hotel bill, either. I've already taken care of that."

She opened her mouth to object, but he shook his head. "No," he said. "Let me do this for you, please. Not because I'm trying to buy anything, but because I want to do it."

It was time to be gracious. "Thank you."

"I wish I didn't have to go."

"Your work is important. You told me yourself, you can't keep on putting it off. And in any case, what's happening in my life right now . . . well—" she stifled a sigh "—it's better that I deal with it alone."

She would miss him, of course, but, if Bennet had some emotional housecleaning to do, so had she. She needed time to come to terms with the fact that, regardless of what she'd been telling herself, she loved him. She knew, if she were to press him now, she could sweep aside his reservations; that her present vulnerability brought out all his protective instincts. But that would be settling for second best. She'd done that once already, believing that she had love enough for two, and it was not a mistake she would ever repeat. If she and Bennet were to have any sort of future together, it would have to be one based on mutual need and commitment.

"I know I've misjudged you in the past, Maggie, that I hurt you with my accusations," he said, tuning in on her thoughts with uncanny accuracy. "It was wrong and stupid of me, and I don't want to hurt you a second time. I don't know how long I'll be gone, but when I do come back I promise—"

"Don't!" She touched her fingers to his lips. She wanted so much to hear him say only the right words. "Please don't make promises you might not keep."

"I won't." He wound the strand of hair a little tighter. "May I kiss you goodbye?"

Her throat was clogged with tears again. There seemed to be no end to them. She closed her eyes to hide her distress. The touch of his lips, warm and sweet, was something she wanted to imprint forever on her memory.

"Send me away, Maggie," he whispered against her mouth.

She gathered very ounce of discipline at her command and hammered it to her will. "Good night, Bennet. Safe journey." Then she turned her key in the lock, slipped inside the room, and shut out temptation before it broke her heart again.

During the days that followed, Maggie discovered that nature had a way of insulating a person from total collapse by numbing the senses. She went through all the motions expected of her, spending her days at the hospital, dealing with Eric, and returning to the hotel each night. It all came to an end when, a week to the day after Bennet had left for Europe, Wendy died. Maggie stayed for the memorial service out of respect and love for her friend, ignoring the cold hostility of Eric and his father. Bennet had been right. How they felt about her didn't matter.

Her impressions of that week were hazy. Aside from her sadness, her overriding feeling was one of utter exhaustion. She supposed it was caused by stress, and that it would ease once Bennet came home and she knew where she was headed with her life.

She returned to Sagepointe the day before school began and stopped by the big house to visit Chris and Mrs. Marshall. Beau heard her footsteps and came racing around the side of the house, tail thrashing in welcome. Chris showed her his new school clothes and the crayons and blunt-nosed scissors that he'd be using in class. And Mrs. Marshall told her that Bennet had extended his overseas trip to include eastern Europe. The last time he'd phoned he thought he'd be gone a couple of extra weeks.

CHAPTER TWELVE

BENNET sent postcards with photographs of magnificent old buildings and baroque concert halls, from faraway places like Prague, Budapest, Bucharest, Sophia, but the messages were the kind that anyone could read—and probably did. In Sagepointe, mail not enclosed in an envelope was considered fair game for public examination. Once, he phoned, but the connection was so poor that it was like talking to a stranger, and no more satisfying than the cards. His name was in the news.

"Bennet Montgomery, world-renowned orchestral director...international ambassador of music...negotiating concert appearance for artists who've never before performed in the western world.'

It was history in the making as sweeping government changes in eastern Europe opened up new cultural opportunities for him. Two weeks became three, and then a month.

Was it greater freedom to travel that kept him away, Maggie wondered, or his personal odyssey?

School kept her busy. From Monday to Friday she devoted all her energies to her class, grateful that the exuberant nine-year-olds left her no time to dwell on her personal heartaches. At the weekends she drove herself to the limits of her endurance, preparing projects for the upcoming week, coaching the junior gymnastics team, helping to make costumes for the Christmas pageant.

Whenever she could, she spent time with Chris. His adjustment to school was not turning out as well as she'd hoped. Although his learning ability was above average, his social skills were poor. More than once other staff members expressed concern about his behavior. He was disruptive in class, demanding more than his share of attention. He was aggressive in the schoolyard, picking fights with other children. Too many sudden changes at home had undermined his security. He clung to Maggie, and it broke her heart that she had to keep him at a distance. For both their sakes, she had to try to lessen his dependence on her, and found herself resenting Bennet for keeping both her and the child in limbo like this.

September became October. The days grew shorter. The onset of cold weather fringed the lake with ice and stripped the trees of leaves. As far as possible, Maggie avoided social contact with people in Sagepointe. She knew they were curious about Bennet. He'd assumed a new glamour and they looked to her for personal details not found in the newspapers. But it was better not to talk about him, not to think about him. It was best to be so busy that there wasn't time to wonder if he ever talked or thought about her.

John Keyes disapproved mightily of the way she was conducting her life. "How long do you think you can keep this up?" he demanded, cornering her one day during the lunch hour, when all the other teachers were relaxing in the staff room and she was at her desk, marking assignments she should have dealt with at the weekend.

"Keep what up?" she asked, totaling a score and reaching for the next exercise book.

"This grueling schedule you've set for yourself." John spread his hand over the page in front of her, his broad palm and splayed fingers covering the work she was trying to grade, and forced her to concentrate all her attention on him. "Maggie, you're not here anymore."

"Well, of course I'm here," she retorted irritably. "Who else do you think stands in front of my class every day?"

"That's not what I meant and you know it."

Unfortunately, she did. She was a physical presence only. She was shutting down on her emotions, afraid that if she didn't she'd want and hope for more than Bennet could deliver. There'd been so much anger between them, so much distrust, and only a little tenuous hope for better things to come. The longer he was gone the more his absence eroded her confidence. He was never coming back, she decided. He'd forgotten her. He didn't care enough. He had no room for her in his life.

"I'm dealing with a lot, John," she said. "I've been very worried and upset about my former mother-in-law—"

"Put all that behind you and start worrying about yourself," he interrupted with brusque affection. "You're heading for a breakdown, the way you're going. What amazes me is that you ought to look like hell, but somehow you don't. I guess youth and good looks go a long way toward covering up a person's real state of health."

It was that strange, backhanded compliment that woke her up, quite literally, and put her in touch with life again. Beyond a sort of peripheral gratitude that it chugged along on minimal maintenance, she hadn't paid real attention to her body in weeks, but John's words seemed to act as a catalyst on her subconscious, hauling her out of sleep that night to the flashing perception that, physically, she was different from the way she used to be.

Considering all the other things preying on her mind, she supposed she could be forgiven for not having noticed sooner the symptoms she had long ago stopped expecting would ever be hers to discover. Once acknowledged, however, they refused to be ignored, and she didn't need a doctor to confirm her own belated conclusions. That sort of corroboration was superfluous beside the truth of a woman's deepest instinct.

Bennet had been quite wrong when he'd said, that evening in Long Island, that it was as well their affair had ended before any great harm had been done. By then she had already conceived his child. Two months later she knew that with unshakable certainty.

The realization shocked her out of her emotional limbo with a stabbing, pins-and-needles sort of awakening of the senses that overwhelmed her. At one o'clock in the morning she lay wide-awake in her bed, exploring the gentle convex curve of her abdomen with tentative, curious hands. From complete ignorance she was flung into such total awareness of her condition that she was sure she could feel the exact spot where her baby slept, and was half convinced that, if her own pulse would thud a little less turbulently, she'd be able to hear a second, more delicate heartbeat.

The moment of discovery was so thrilling that she was astonished, long hours later, to find tears had gathered like rows of tiny seed pearls about to slip loose from her eyelashes. She didn't know why she was crying. She felt neither sadness nor anger nor despair, only wonder and a deep gratitude that, despite what she'd been conditioned to believe during her marriage to Eric, having a baby was something she *could* do, after all.

The next day euphoria gave way to reality. She was an unmarried schoolteacher in a very small town. Eventually her pregnancy would become apparent to the most unobservant eye. Even allowing for more liberal attitudes toward single parents, she knew she had no choice but to resign her position at the school. A person in her position was expected to set standards and examples. Producing a child with no evidence of a father to complete the family picture simply wasn't an acceptable alternative, quite apart from the speculation that was bound to arise once word of her situation leaked out.

Telling Bennet was out of the question. He'd do the honorable thing, and she didn't want him on those terms. She'd made the brave promise, back at the start of the summer, that she'd never try to lasso him into a relationship he didn't want. She wasn't about to use the oldest trick in the world to snag him now. Either he came back to her of his own accord, or not at all.

That afternoon she handed in her notice for the second time, and made it plain that nothing John said or did would change her mind. She was leaving her job at Christmas with or without his blessing. "For health reasons," she insisted, and, after surveying her narrowly for some time without saying a word, he shrugged and slipped her letter into an inside pocket of his jacket.

At the beginning of November, parent-teacher conferences took place at the school, beginning at six in the evening. It had been bitterly cold all week, and at about four o'clock that afternoon it began to snow. Maggie was glad winter had come early. It gave her a reason to dress in a bulky, hip-length loose-fitting sweater and full skirt that hid her thickening middle. Bad enough that word of her leaving had leaked out, without everyone guessing why.

Normally she looked forward to her interviews. She'd always believed that the friendly cooperation and communication between teachers and parents made for better interaction with the children, but this year personal anxieties overshadowed her usual enjoyment.

On top of that, the sleepiness which she now recognized as one of the symptoms of early pregnancy still plagued her. She supposed it was easier to deal with than morning sickness, but by the time her last interview ended she felt too weary to join everyone else for coffee and dessert in the gym. All she wanted was to go home and climb into bed.

She didn't hear her classroom door open again, didn't have the vaguest idea she was no longer alone, because she had her back turned and was busy writing the next day's date and lesson order on the blackboard. Her first intimation that she had another visitor was the sound of someone clearing his throat, and her initial reaction was one of pure annoyance.

Then he spoke, and all the blood rushed to her feet, leaving her so weak that the chalk scraped down the blackboard, setting her teeth achingly on edge before it slipped from her fingers and went skittering across the floor.

"Miss Jones," he said, in a deep, familiar baritone, "I don't have an appointment, but I wonder if you'd spare me a few moments of your time anyway?"

In all those old romantic movies Maggie had loved to watch when she was a teenager, unseen violins rose to a crescendo at this point, and there was never any doubt about what came next. The hero would be standing there, arms held wide, and the heroine would float into them, graceful as a dancer, all her doubts and miseries swept away like shadows in the moonlight.

Reality was much less kind. The overhead striplighting glared down, brutally exposing. All the fatigue, all the loneliness and uncertainty seemed to manifest themselves in sagging lines on her face, making her feel old and ugly when she needed most desperately to appear lovely and composed. Leadfooted with shock, she grabbed clumsily at her chair, which was not quite where she thought it would be. Even her voice betrayed her. "You've come back," she croaked.

"Yes."

She hardly dared phrase her next question. "Why?"

He spread those beautiful hands before him, palms up, commanding attention. "I need your help," he said simply.

She would not look at him, even though she could feel his eyes burning into hers. "Why?" she asked, again.

"Because I'm in serious trouble, and you came to my rescue once before."

Her mind seemed fastened on irrelevancies. "How did you know where to find me?" As if it mattered!

He took a step closer, and Maggie's heart slammed wildly in her throat. "Edith Caverley told me. She saw a car outside your house, heard someone banging on your front door." Amusement filtered rustily through his voice, as though it had been a long time since he'd found occasion to laugh. "She thought it her civic duty to investigate."

He brought the breath of winter, clean and pure, into the overheated room, banishing the stale smell of chalk and poster paint and sneakers. Without permission, her eyes strayed to his face and, once there, feasted on the sight of him. Diamond-studded snowflakes sprinkled his hair and his fine black worsted overcoat, paradoxically calling up the memory of that summer morning she'd found him waiting on her front porch. He no more belonged now than he had then.

Still her gaze clung. Had he always been so tall, so elegantly lean and handsome? Were his lashes always so dense and silky, his cheekbones so sharply defined, his mouth so invitingly tender?

Emotions rushed upon her, frighteningly intense. Why was it, she wondered, crumpling onto her chair, that she could sail through the first two months of pregnancy without a single disagreeable symptom, and then, when she was well into her third month and supposedly past such unpleasantness, nausea threatened to embarrass her in front of Bennet, of all people?

He was watching her, examining her every feature with grave concern. "Maggie, are you ill?"

The way he spoke her name turned it into a caress, a lovely intimacy that hinted at all sorts of foolish, forbidden things. Like love and joy and happy-ever-after.

She shook her head and she was appalled at the dizziness that assailed her. "No," she said in a thin, old-lady's voice. "What do you mean, you need help?"

He sighed, then, and looked at his hands, his lashes sweeping darkly down to hide his eyes. But she saw his mouth tighten, scored on either side by grooves that hadn't been there a minute ago, which made him look suddenly haggard and much older. "I'm a desperate man," he explained, "and if you turn me away I don't know what I'm going to do."

It was so much a repeat of their first meeting that she ought to have been able to endure it, except that something had changed since early summer. The arrogance and certainty were gone, replaced by a much more treacherous humility.

"Is it Christopher?" she asked, and only by the most tearing sort of control did she prevent herself from begging, Please say it's not. Please need me for your sake, not his.

A glimmer of that charming smile ghosted over his features. "Well, he *is* very annoyed that he's not in your class. He misses you... but not nearly as much as *I* miss you." Wretched unhappiness carved his face once more, and, shoving his way past the neat rows of small desks, he came to lean over her. "Maggie, I know I've been gone a long time, much longer than I ever intended. Please don't punish me by sending me away empty-handed."

How easily he tapped her sympathy. Almost as easily as he'd walked away from her just over eight weeks ago, she reminded herself, struggling to remain unmoved. They had been among the longest and hardest weeks of her life. She had to be sure the bad times were over before she allowed herself to hope again. "And now that you're back, what is it you want from me?"

"Whatever you feel able to give."

A baby, perhaps? For one delirious second Maggie thought she'd uttered the words out loud, and clapped a hand to her mouth. He was much too close, and if she allowed him to touch her, heaven alone knew what she might not say or do.

She needed to get out of this too bright, too confining room that allowed her no secrets. She needed to hide in the dark outside and draw in great breaths of cold air to clear her head and settle her stomach. She needed time to decide how best to tell him about her pregnancy.

Her coat hung in the corner. Stepping past him, she reached for it and struggled to slip her arms into the sleeves before he could help her. "We can't talk here," she said.

"I know. Will you go for a drive with me?"

And leave herself at his mercy in the intimacy of his car, with the sound of his voice and the scent of leather and sandalwood swirling warmly together, too tempting to resist? Not until she learned if the answers he'd taken so long to find were in tune with her own hopes!

"No, I'd like to walk. I need the exercise."

It was still snowing, fine, dry flakes that settled like feathers on everything they touched, from the topmost branches of the pines to the road leading out of the parking lot. Even the tire tracks of earlier cars were covered.

She turned toward the park, away from her house and Edith's curious eyes. "Now," she said, as the last streetlamp faded into the night and there was only the snow's reflection to witness her discomposure, "why don't you tell me why you've really come back, Bennet?"

"I need a tutor again," he said. "Someone with the patience to deal with a very handicapped student, and naturally, considering your excellent track record, I thought of you, Miss Jones."

CHAPTER THIRTEEN

BENNET stared at the tips of his polished leather boots as he spoke, and for that Maggie was grateful. At least he didn't see her jaw drop in hideous dismay, or realize how much she'd been hoping, in some quiet, tiny recess of an otherwise rational mind, that he would say something breathtakingly romantic, like, I love you. I want to marry you. I'm miserable without you. What good would that have done, after all, when her life had become too complicated for simple new beginnings?

"Will you take the job?" he asked, stuffing his hands deep in the pockets of his coat.

Her eyes were so blurred with tears that she couldn't see where she was stepping. "What if I said you've been gone so long that I grew tired of waiting for you and made other plans?"

"I'd ask what it would take to make you reconsider."

"I don't know," she said, her words as brittle as glass. "To be honest, I feel unconnected from everything that ought to be important to me. Wendy died last month . . ."

At last, a legitimate reason to cry! Her voice wobbled into silence as the tears tracked wetly down her cold face.

"Maggie, I'm so sorry! I should have asked about her sooner."

He made as if to draw her to him in sympathy, but she shook her head and waved him away. She was tempted to explain that the reason she was so emotional was that she was pregnant with his child, but she knew that, for her permanent peace of mind, he had to declare himself first. She would not play on his sympathy or his guilt. "She left me some money," she quavered, "and I thought perhaps the time had come for me to try something different."

"I see."

He lapsed into silence and she stole a bleary glance at him. He had half turned away from her, and was looking about him at the shrubs and benches draped in snow, the proud angle of his head a dark silhouette above her. If he'd decided there wasn't room for a wife in his life, would there ever come a time when she'd forget him enough for the torn place in her heart to mend?

"This job I have in mind would be different," he finally said with soft persuasion. "I'm desperate for someone to take me in hand, to teach me how to laugh, how not to be afraid of happiness. If the world were to end tomorrow, I would die without having properly lived. I'm through with running away, Maggie. I want to come home. I want you."

This time when he tried to touch her she couldn't pull away. One of his hands stole inside the collar of her coat to settle around her neck, while the other reached down to turn her face up to meet his.

"I can't imagine why you want me for this job," she remarked perversely, even though she was on the brink of capitulation. "You've resented me almost from the first day we met."

"Of course I have, my darling! You shook me out of my complacent certainty that I lived in the best of all possible worlds, with enough pleasure to keep me satisfied and few irritations to annoy me. Because of you, I started questioning my values and began to feel cheated. That bright, ambitious future I had mapped out all at once looked terribly empty."

His lips skimmed over her eyes and down her cheek to settle hesitatingly at the corner of her mouth. "That man who thought he knew all the answers suddenly realizd he couldn't find his way out of a brown paper bag without Miss Jones to help him along."

"He sounds like a bit of a fool," she said on a ragged breath.

"He's a first-class jerk, as a matter of fact. I expect it'll take a lifetime to get him sorted out."

"How do I know you won't fire me, or run out on me again?"

"Because I discovered that putting distance between us didn't help me escape you. You came with me, interfering with my business, upsetting my schedules, trespassing into my dreams, undermining everything I set my mind to. For the first time that I can remember, my work failed to enthrall me." He bent his head and nibbled the length of her jaw to her earlobe. "I'm afraid you've ruined me."

Driven to play devil's advocate one more time, Maggie took a fresh attack. "How much has Chris to do with all this?"

"Chris needs you almost as much as I need you. The difference is, he realizd that from the beginning. When I walked in the door this evening, he practically pushed me out again before I could say hello. None of that, 'Hi, Uncle Bennet, gee, it's nice you're home' stuff, just 'Go get Maggie!' " Bennet led her to a bench under the trees, swept it free of snow, and pulled her down beside him. "I tell you, Miss Jones, that boy knows how to persist!"

The first real smile in weeks crept across Maggie's face. "Do I detect signs of battle fatigue already?"

"My darling," he said, resting his forehead against hers, "it's more than my life is worth to go back without you. If you won't marry me for love, at least marry me out of pity."

Her heart almost stopped. *"Marry you?"* she echoed with faint dismay.

"Well, of course," he said. "I thought you understood that."

She understood that he'd tossed out an offhanded proposal of marriage without once telling her that he loved her. A more confident woman might have taken such omission in her stride and drawn her own conclusions, but Maggie's self-assurance had taken a few knocks too many to be so easily satisfied.

She'd never again take love for granted. There was little doubt that she was the ideal candidate to help Bennet bring up Chris, and even less doubt that her baby would be better off with a father, but she wasn't about to settle for a mutually convenient arrangement. If she and Bennet were to be married, it would have to be for all the right reasons.

He sensed her reservations and shook his head wearily. "I spent the whole of last week rehearsing how I was going to say all this, and I still don't have it right, do I? My only excuse is that I don't do this sort of thing very often."

"And why are you doing it now, Bennet?" she asked, knowing she sounded like a disapproving schoolmarm, but unable to help herself.

"Because I need you. I miss you. I'm miserable without you. I know I've behaved abominably some of the time and like a complete fool the rest of the time, and I'll do anything to get you to give me another chance." He picked up her hands and held them close inside his. "Dear Miss Jones, it's obvious to me that I need a lifetime teacher to keep me from constantly screwing up, and it's equally obvious that that person is you. Please say you'll marry me and save my life."

The setting was perfect, a dreamscape of muted sound and gauzy images. Above, the stars pricked through the cloud layer, and only an occasional snowflake still drifted down. Why was she hesitating, when every last inch of her screamed out for her to accept his proposal?

She knew why. "Bennet," she whispered, her throat aching, "what about all those things that got in the way before? You once said I wasn't what you thought

I was, and things are even less what they seem now than they were then. I'm afraid you want a perfection that I can't offer, and that if I disappoint you in any way you'll turn away from me again."

"No," he insisted, drawing her roughly to him, "that's not so! I know we can't wipe out the past, that we can only go forward." He groaned with sudden pain and brought his mouth swooping down on hers. His lips were cold and sweet and desperate, drawing her soul from her to heal deep, hidden wounds within him. "Darling Maggie, all I can tell you is that I've dealt with more devils in the last two months than I thought existed in a lifetime, and the bottom line is that I love you and I'll go on loving you for the rest of my life, no matter what happens. I don't care that I'm not your first love, as long as—"

He loved her! Wells of happiness sprang to life, overriding Maggie's determination to exercise due caution. The blood raced through her veins, bringing warmth and joy to every last neglected corner. "As long as what?" she murmured, in thrall to the pulsing rhythm of a heart gone mad.

He traced the arch of her eyebrow with a scrupulously tender finger. "As long as I'm your last."

"You always did drive a hard bargain," she whispered, as fresh tears trembled along her lashes. "I suppose you want me to give you an answer right now?"

"Naturally," he replied with a trace of his old arrogance. "We've wasted enough time already. We should have been married before now, and starting a family of our own.''

Maggie knew there would never be a better time to tell him. ''Well,'' she said, swallowing the knot of apprehension that rose in her throat, ''it just so happens that, as far as the last goes, we already are.''

He grew very still, and so quiet that she could almost hear the stars crackle frostily in the heavens. Please let this be happy news, she begged him silently.

He withdrew along the bench far enough to be able to look her over from head to toe. ''We are?''

She nodded, and, taking his hand, placed it between the folds of her coat and rested it against her once-slender waist.

He tested the feel of her with startled, experimental fingers. ''A baby?'' he whispered, as though he was afraid he might disturb it if he spoke too loudly. ''Are you sure?''

''Yes. I saw a doctor in Annisville.''

Bennet digested the news for long, nerve-racking minutes, then inspected her through narrowed eyes. ''Is that why you agreed to marry me?'' he asked at last.

It wasn't the time to point out that, technically, she hadn't agreed, not yet. ''Would it matter, if I had?''

He snatched his hand away. ''Yes! I have to come first!''

The tears spilled over again, mixed with laughter. He would always be impossible! ''Oh, Bennet, as if there's any doubt about that!''

"Well," he said plaintively, "you've never actually come right out and told me that you love me."

"I love you."

He wiped away her tears and asked with endearing humility, "And will you marry me?"

"I'll marry you."

"Right away?" Deliberately, he unbuttoned her coat and his, then drew her hard against him. How perfectly the baby fitted between them, safe in her warmth, supported against his strength.

"Yes," she murmured, pulling his head down so that she could kiss him. "Tomorrow, if you like."

"Oh, Lord!" he groaned, settling his mouth against hers, "Edith Caverley will have a field day with this little morsel of gossip. Do you suppose I could convince you to move to some place a little less... convivial? I'm really not cut out for small-town living, after all."

"I can be happy anywhere, as long as we're together."

"I was thinking about some place not too far from an international airport, like Toronto. When I have to go on tour, I'd like to have you with me, but if you feel you should be at home—" he rested his hand again on their unborn child "—well, I want to be able to catch a direct flight back, to you and ours. It wouldn't be quite the same as Sagepointe, but we could buy a big house in some nice, outlying suburb, something with a big garden and lots of trees to make it feel like the country—"

"With room for the children to play with Beau."

"Darling Miss Jones," Bennet murmured, with fatal, irresistible charm, "you always were so sensible. No wonder I love you so much!"

POSTCARDS FROM EUROPE

HARLEQUIN PRESENTS®

Hi—

Have arrived safely in Germany, but Diether von Lössingen denies that he's the baby's father. Am determined that he shoulder his responsibilities!

Love, Sophie

P.S. Diether's shoulders are certainly wide enough.

**Fifty red-blooded, white-hot, true-blue hunks
from every State in the Union!**

Look for MEN MADE IN AMERICA! Written by some
of our most poplar authors, these stories feature fifty of
the strongest, sexiest men, each from a different state in
the union!

Two titles available every other month at your favorite
retail outlet.

In March, look for:

TANGLED LIES by Anne Stuart (Hawaii)
ROGUE'S VALLEY by Kathleen Creighton (Idaho)

In May, look for:

LOVE BY PROXY by Diana Palmer (Illinois)
POSSIBLES by Lass Small (Indiana)

You won't be able to resist MEN MADE IN AMERICA!

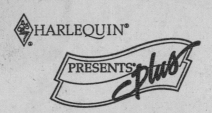

My Valentine

1994

Celebrate the most romantic day of the year with
MY VALENTINE 1994
a collection of original stories, written by
four of Harlequin's most popular authors...

MARGOT DALTON
MURIEL JENSEN
MARISA CARROLL
KAREN YOUNG

*Available in February, wherever
Harlequin Books are sold.*

HARLEQUIN ®

VAL94

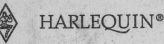

HARLEQUIN®

Don't miss these Harlequin favorites by some of our most distinguished authors!
And now, you can receive a discount by ordering two or more titles!

HT#25409	THE NIGHT IN SHINING ARMOR by JoAnn Ross	$2.99	☐
HT#25471	LOVESTORM by JoAnn Ross	$2.99	☐
HP#11463	THE WEDDING by Emma Darcy	$2.89	☐
HP#11592	THE LAST GRAND PASSION by Emma Darcy	$2.99	☐
HR#03188	DOUBLY DELICIOUS by Emma Goldrick	$2.89	☐
HR#03248	SAFE IN MY HEART by Leigh Michaels	$2.89	☐
HS#70464	CHILDREN OF THE HEART by Sally Garrett	$3.25	☐
HS#70524	STRING OF MIRACLES by Sally Garrett	$3.39	☐
HS#70500	THE SILENCE OF MIDNIGHT by Karen Young	$3.39	☐
HI#22178	SCHOOL FOR SPIES by Vickie York	$2.79	☐
HI#22212	DANGEROUS VINTAGE by Laura Pender	$2.89	☐
HI#22219	TORCH JOB by Patricia Rosemoor	$2.89	☐
HAR#16459	MACKENZIE'S BABY by Anne McAllister	$3.39	☐
HAR#16466	A COWBOY FOR CHRISTMAS by Anne McAllister	$3.39	☐
HAR#16462	THE PIRATE AND HIS LADY by Margaret St. George	$3.39	☐
HAR#16477	THE LAST REAL MAN by Rebecca Flanders	$3.39	☐
HH#28704	A CORNER OF HEAVEN by Theresa Michaels	$3.99	☐
HH#28707	LIGHT ON THE MOUNTAIN by Maura Seger	$3.99	☐

Harlequin Promotional Titles

#83247	YESTERDAY COMES TOMORROW by Rebecca Flanders	$4.99	☐
#83257	MY VALENTINE 1993	$4.99	☐
	(short-story collection featuring Anne Stuart, Judith Arnold, Anne McAllister, Linda Randall Wisdom)		

(limited quantities available on certain titles)

	AMOUNT	$
DEDUCT:	**10% DISCOUNT FOR 2+ BOOKS**	$
ADD:	**POSTAGE & HANDLING**	$
	($1.00 for one book, 50¢ for each additional)	
	APPLICABLE TAXES*	$ _____
	TOTAL PAYABLE	$ _____
	(check or money order—please do not send cash)	

To order, complete this form and send it, along with a check or money order for the total above, payable to Harlequin Books, to: **In the U.S.:** 3010 Walden Avenue, P.O. Box 9047, Buffalo, NY 14269-9047; **In Canada:** P.O. Box 613, Fort Erie, Ontario, L2A 5X3.

Name: _____

Address: _____ City: _____

State/Prov.: _____ Zip/Postal Code: _____

*New York residents remit applicable sales taxes.
Canadian residents remit applicable GST and provincial taxes.

HBACK-JM